Z-TOWN

Praise for Eden Darry

The House

"Eden Darry is on my to-watch list. I am eagerly anticipating her new release because I adored this one so much. The pacing was excellent; combining the thriller stalker with the haunted house was a stroke of genius causing threats from both sides and really putting the pressure on…If you have loved *The Shining, The Haunting of Hill House* (TV show), or *The Amityville Horror* then you should absolutely get this book. Eden Darry wrote a wonderful horror. It was exciting, captivating and had me on the edge of my seat with anticipation."—*Lesbian Review*

"For a debut novel, Eden Darry did really well. This book had everything a modern-day horror novel needed. A modern couple, a haunted house, and a talented author to combine the two. The atmosphere was eerie and the plot held a lot of suspense. The couple went between love and hate, and if only they had talked to one another! And the reader just kept turning those pages."—*Kat Loves Books*

"A solid debut that is creepy and intense."—*Lez Review Books*

Vanished

"*Vanished* by Eden Darry is a postapocalyptic horror that I thoroughly enjoyed. If you love stories where people have to survive against huge odds, postapocalyptic, end of the world kind of stories, then this is a must-read. If you love stories where something bad is lurking in the background being just sinister enough to make your skin crawl, then this is an awesome read."—*Lesbian Review*

"I really do like Darry's writing—she creates a great ominous atmosphere in her narrative. The initial chapters with the storm perfectly set the stage for what is to come. There's also a suitably unnerving and creepy feel as Loveday begins to realize that there is no one else in the village and a nice bit of tension while she and Ellery are searching houses."—*C-Spot Reviews*

By the Author

The House

Vanished

Z-Town

Visit us at www.boldstrokesbooks.com

Z-Town

by
Eden Darry

2020

Z-TOWN

ISBN 13: 978-1-63555-743-5

THIS TRADE PAPERBACK ORIGINAL IS PUBLISHED BY
BOLD STROKES BOOKS, INC.
P.O. BOX 249
VALLEY FALLS, NY 12185

FIRST EDITION: OCTOBER 2020

CREDITS
EDITOR: RUTH STERNGLANTZ
PRODUCTION DESIGN: STACIA SEAMAN
COVER DESIGN BY JEANINE HENNING

Acknowledgments

I'd like to thank Radclyffe and Sandy for publishing me again and for being on board with the idea of zombies in Provincetown.

Ruth for always being super patient and an amazing editor.

And Catherine. For the hours you spent reading through the first drafts, gently encouraging, suggesting, and questioning. I love you.

Lastly, I've tried to stay factual with the geography of Ptown. But those who know the place may spot a couple of inaccuracies. I hope you'll forgive the minor liberties I've taken.

For Catherine

PROLOGUE

The insistent bleeping of the bulldozer almost drowned out the workmen's cries. But Craig, the operator, a great big burly guy who barely fit in the cab, couldn't find his headphones this morning, and they usually drowned out the growl of engines—and any other noise too. Not that Provincetown was a noisy place, at least not in the off season. Even so, without his headphones, Craig knew he would end up with a pounding headache by the end of the day if he was forced to listen to the sounds of the construction site.

The foreman on-site, Steve, gave him shit about it all the time, said it was dangerous if he couldn't hear what was going on around him. Craig told Steve *he* should try to listen to that noise every damn day instead of sitting in his cosy office. Then let him say it was dangerous. Asshole.

As it was he didn't have them on today, so he killed the engine and climbed out of the cab. He went over to where two other guys and Joanne, who sometimes worked with their crew, were gesturing excitedly and pointing. He looked down into the ditch he'd just been digging out. Well, shit. It really *was* something. A box. Not a big box—it was about three feet by three feet—and it looked old.

Craig climbed down into the ditch.

"Don't you think we should call the boss? It might be a body or something," one of the guys who'd found it said.

Craig looked up. "Hell no. It ain't a body. And even if it is, it's been down here a long time. It'll be bones by now. I'm going to look. Fuck the boss—I dug it up, I should be the one who sees what it is."

Craig flicked up the catches on the box. They opened easier than he thought they would considering how long it must have been buried. He pushed up the lid, half expecting a body like the guy said, but it wasn't. What it was was going to make Craig fucking rich.

There were a bunch of broken pots and some cloth that had rotted away until it was just scraps. But there was also jewellery. Gold and silver. And a couple knives that looked like weapons.

"Hey, don't touch that," Craig said as Joanne reached into the box and picked up one of the pieces of jewellery.

"Ouch—damn, Craig. You made me cut myself," Joanne said and pulled her hand back.

"It's only a little cut—don't be a baby. And don't touch my stuff," Craig said.

Craig turned his attention back to the box and grinned.

Finders keepers, which meant no more construction sites and no more bulldozers for him.

Chapter One

L ane Boyd took her seat. Her knees were pressed up against the chair in front, and once again she wished she'd flown business instead of economy—or cattle, as most people called it, and she could see why. This was the new her. Not relying on family money. Being more real, more like everyone else.

Admittedly, her family money paid for this ticket too, but she didn't have a job yet, to be able to buy one with her own money, and everyone had to start somewhere. This was the first step. She'd even written a list, which was currently stuffed somewhere in her carry-on luggage, but she knew it by heart. Step one was get Meg back.

Lane could pinpoint the exact moment she decided she wanted more for her life, and it was the first time she laid eyes on Meg Daltry at a basement club in Soho. Lane had been coming upstairs to smoke a cigarette, thinking about leaving because the place was dead. She got halfway up the stairs when Meg appeared in the doorway.

She'd moved to the side to let Meg pass and immediately knew she was going back down after her smoke. Meg was beautiful. Lane didn't think Meg had even noticed her as she walked by with her eyes lowered, but she'd thanked Lane for moving.

Lane quickly finished her smoke and hurried back downstairs. The club was small with no natural light. The DJ hadn't arrived yet, so old pop tunes were being pumped through the speakers.

She made her way to the empty bar and looked around. There she was. Sitting at a table by herself, sipping a glass of wine. Lane ordered a bottle of beer, gave herself a silent mini pep talk, and walked over.

"Hi," she said. "I'm Lane."

"Meg." Meg smiled and held out her hand.

Lane shook it. It was small and soft and an effort to let it go again.

"Do you mind if I sit down?" she asked. "Or are you waiting for someone?"

Meg shook her head. "I'm not waiting for anyone—you can sit down."

Lane sat and took a drink from her bottle. "You're American—I mean, from the United States?"

"I am."

"Okay, good, because some Canadians get really annoyed when you mistake them for USA-type Americans." Lane gave Meg her hundred-watt smile. It was usually a winner with women.

Meg laughed but it sounded polite rather than genuine. Tone the smile down. *Lane didn't want to look too cocky.*

"Are you from here?" Meg gestured with her glass. "London, I mean."

"I am indeed. Born and raised. If you're after a tour guide, I'm available." Lane smiled again but kept it to about seventy watts. That seemed to go down better.

"I'm sure you are. I'll bet you're a well-known tour guide around here."

Lane's smile faltered. Women usually found her pretty

charming. This was new. Lane wasn't so conceited she couldn't tell Meg wasn't interested in her.

"Look, I saw you upstairs and I thought you were beautiful, so I wanted to come and talk to you. If you want me to go away, I will. No hard feelings," Lane said.

"You know, I'm being kind of rude. You're full of yourself, but that's no reason to be impolite," Meg said. "I'm sorry."

"Full of myself?" Lane laughed. This woman was unusual.

"Your lines seem well practised. Maybe it's a Brit thing. I don't know." Meg shrugged.

Lane took a deep breath. Ordinarily, if a woman clearly wasn't interested, she'd walk away. It didn't matter all that much to her. But there was something about Meg that made her want to keep trying.

"How about we start again? I'll refrain from giving you my usual lines, and you ease up on me. What do you say?" Lane smiled again, but to her surprise this one felt hopeful on her lips. And maybe a little unsure.

Meg seemed to think for a moment. Then she smiled too. "Deal. You want another drink?"

Lane's heart hurt at the memory. Things could have turned out so differently. She sighed and rifled in the seat pouch in front. She pulled out a dog-eared flight magazine with a weird brown stain on the cover and flicked through it. Maybe she should get some perfume to give Meg. Or some jewellery—perhaps a watch. Meg was a stickler for timekeeping, so she might appreciate it. But perhaps not.

When they first started dating, she'd bought Meg a Tiffany bracelet. Meg went all weird and refused to accept it. She'd told Lane it was too much. Lane tried to explain her family were loaded and the bracelet was a drop in the ocean. Meg still refused, and then they'd gotten in a big argument about money and value and other things to do with finances that Lane didn't understand. What she did understand was that Meg had a chip on her shoulder about wealth.

Lane stuffed the magazine back in the seat pouch. Maybe not a present, then. She drummed her fingers on the armrest. God, this was boring. She hated waiting for things, and take-off was usually painful. When she flew business or first, she didn't have to get on the plane for ages. But she was flying cattle today, and apparently, they got on about eight hours before everyone else. It was ridiculous.

Lane grabbed the attention of a passing flight attendant. "Excuse me, do you have any magazines or newspapers or something?"

The flight attendant looked at her like she'd just scraped her off her shoe. "No. There's a magazine in the seat pouch."

Before Lane could say anything else, the flight attendant walked off. Rude.

"Excuse me, do you want this?" A woman in the next aisle over offered her a newspaper. "It's a week old, but I just found it in my flight bag and was going to throw it out. It's online too. They found some Viking treasure in Ptown last week, and they update the story all the time. It's pretty interesting if you like that sort of thing."

Lane didn't.

"Thank you." She leaned forward and took the newspaper from the woman. The *Outer Cape Echo*. "This is where you're from?" she asked the woman.

"I am. Have you been?" the woman asked.

"No, but I'm on my way there."

"Oh, well, I'm sure you'll love it. We're biased, but it's a great little town. We've just been visiting our daughter in London, and we can't wait to get home."

Lane nodded and leaned back in her seat. She didn't want

to carry the conversation on, although she was tempted to ask about Meg. From what she'd heard, Provincetown was tiny, so there was a good chance this woman knew her. But that would mean more conversation—possibly for the whole flight—and Lane didn't want to chance it.

She'd read the newspaper, though. It was something to do, and she was headed to the town. Lane unfolded it and started to read.

VIKING TREASURE FOUND ON WINTHROP STREET

PROVINCETOWN—Yesterday morning when contractors showed up to work, the last thing they expected to find was Viking treasure. The haul, stored in an original Viking chest, was uncovered by Craig Cherry. "At first we thought maybe there was a dead body inside. I opened it up and found all this old stuff. Didn't know what it was, but it looked like it might be worth a few bucks."

And Craig was right. Provincetown Historical Society's Wendy Moon believes the treasure to be definitive proof that Thorvold Eriksson docked his longboats in Provincetown Harbour in 1007. The haul still has to be assessed by experts from Boston, but if Moon is right, this could be a significant discovery for Provincetown.

If you want to take a look at the Viking treasure, then head along to Provincetown Public Library where it's on display. There's something for everyone, with jewellery and weapons, including a Viking seax, or fighting knife.

Meg Daltry checked her watch. Three hours until closing. For once she was glad about that. She'd have worked a fourteen hour shift today by the time she finished at the bar, and she knew she'd be dead on her feet. The only thing that kept her going the last couple hours was the thought of hot tea, her couch, and the baseball highlights.

They were in the run-up to Women's Week, and Provincetown was starting to fill up again. Not that it ever really stopped filling up from spring until fall, but usually there was a short lull between the high summer season and the fall events, culminating in Christmas. Not this time. And despite the weather, people kept right on coming. It was good though—good for the Squealing Pig at least, not so good for her feet, which currently throbbed in her sneakers.

During her year abroad to London last year, she didn't remember her feet aching quite so much, and the pub she'd worked at was just as busy as the Squealing Pig. She guessed it was age—and that was a depressing thought. It seemed like yesterday she'd been twenty-five and full of dreams about opening her own bar. Now she was thirty-two and still working for someone else, and that hadn't been the plan at all.

She'd scrimped and saved so she could spend two whole years in London, learning all she could about authentic British pubs, before launching her own bar. But when her brother got sick, Meg flew home from London early and used all the money she'd saved for his medical bills. Now she was starting from scratch. Again. Not that she minded—her brother was more important than any bar. But it meant she'd be closer to forty by the time she opened her own place.

"Hey, Meg, put another in there, would you?" Dana Sheedy held up her glass and smiled.

Dana was a paramedic and owned one of the bed and breakfast places in town as well. She came in every night for exactly two beers. She'd stay two hours—one for each beer—then head home. Every night was the same. Meg liked her. She'd been in Provincetown forever.

"Sure, Dana. How are you doing? How's your hand?" Meg grabbed a clean glass and poured Dana her second beer.

"It's not too bad. I've come down with a cold since, though. Joanne can't stop apologizing. I told her a million times—stop saying sorry."

"I guess she feels bad. Did she say why she bit you?" Meg asked.

"Nah. She can't explain it. Said she just came over funny. I sent her to the hospital in Hyannis for a blood test. That stuff she cut herself on at the construction site was old. Might be she got some kind of infection, I don't know. I guess I'm a little run down too, which is making me feel worse. We've got a full house this month, so it'd better be gone by next week."

Meg put Dana's beer on the bar and totalled up her tab. Not that it took much work when she always drank the same thing. Meg had given up convincing her to try their monthly guest beer. That had been Meg's idea, and it was popular. A ton of pubs in London did it and it really boosted sales.

"Well, I hope so too. Once the weather clears up, I bet you'll feel a whole lot better."

Dana nodded and sipped her beer. She turned her attention back to the game on the screen above the bar. "Yeah," she said. "It's been pretty bad this last week. So dark and cold for this time of year. Days seem shorter right now. Weird."

And she was right, Meg thought. The sun hadn't come out for a week it seemed, and the nights came in earlier than they should this time of year. Probably global warming or something. Meg grabbed a bunch of glasses off the bar and put them in the dishwasher. The weather reminded her of winter in London. She smiled. That was a fun year. Well, almost year.

Just like it always did when she thought of London, Meg's mind went to Lane. She'd been fun too. Not someone Meg would date seriously, but she was hot and really sweet. Lane was also childish and aimless with way too much money. Long-term, she would have driven Meg crazy. Meg still thought about her, though, and she wondered about that. What they'd had certainly wasn't some great love affair, but Lane had stuck in Meg's mind. Which was stupid. They were a horrible match. So why couldn't Meg put Lane out of her mind? Especially when Lane had probably forgotten all about her.

When Meg broke it off, Lane hadn't seemed bothered at all. Truth be told, it stung Meg's ego just a little. It was for the best, though. Meg was always going to come back to the United States, and it wasn't as if she and Lane had been going anywhere in a romantic sense. Even if she *had* thought about them being more, the way Lane accepted Meg finishing things between them told Meg everything she needed to know about how Lane saw their relationship.

Meg had never been one for relationships anyway. She'd dated on and off over the years, but the idea of settling down hadn't ever been in the forefront of her mind. She wondered if there was something wrong with her, or if she just hadn't met the right woman yet.

Even if briefly, Meg wondered whether Lane could be that person.

When they'd met, something sparked inside her. A tiny flame caught. But then she got to know Lane a little better and realized they weren't well suited at all. So she'd squashed the flame and concentrated on having a good time instead. Although sometimes, when they were curled up on the couch, Meg had let herself daydream about herself and Lane as something more.

But that was stupid. Just a daydream. Lane had been a

lot of fun. She'd made Meg feel lighter. Probably because she was such a damn child. And boy had she made Meg laugh. But Lane had shown clearly that she wasn't cut out for anything more.

❖

"What do you get if you cross a joke and a rhetorical question?"

Meg and Lane were still lying in bed at three p.m., and Meg didn't feel even a little bad about it. This was new for her. She wasn't used to being so lazy.

Meg rolled over and faced Lane. "I don't know. What do you get if you cross a joke and a rhetorical question?" she asked.

Lane stayed silent, grinned at Meg, and wiggled her eyebrows.

"What? Oh. That's a stupid joke." Meg laughed. "Where do you get them?"

"You don't like my jokes?" Lane made a sad face.

"You know I don't." Meg poked her in the side and moved closer. "I put up with them because you're great in bed. Most of the time, I just tune you out."

Lane burst out laughing. "That's really mean. I feel used."

"You should feel used," Meg joked and tilted her head for a kiss.

Lane obliged. Meg sighed at the feel of Lane's soft lips against hers. She really was a great kisser. And Meg was having a great day. "I like you, Lane." The words came out before she could stop them.

Lane gripped Meg's chin gently and kissed the corner of her mouth. "I like you too. Very much."

"I think we should stay here, in this bed, forever." Meg

knew she couldn't and probably wouldn't want to, but right now, everything seemed so perfect. She didn't want it to end.

❖

"Meg? Hey, Meg."

Meg was jolted back to the present. "Sorry, Wendy, I was totally in my own world."

"Don't worry about it, honey. You must be exhausted. You were working when I came in here at lunch."

Wendy Moon was the local historian and owned a souvenir store on Whalers Wharf. It mostly sold knock-off Viking artifacts that didn't seem to have much to do with Provincetown, but Wendy made it work. Meg was pretty sure she was a professor of something, but she couldn't remember what. "We're short-staffed right now, and it's good money, so I don't mind. What can I get you?"

"White wine please. Joanne still out sick?"

Meg nodded. "Three days now. Must be pretty bad because she never calls in sick. She needs the money. I don't know how she does it. Working construction during the day and here at night."

"She works hard, for sure. I guess she needs to with a little girl to feed. Is she sick too?"

"Lois? Why would she be sick? Joanne cut herself. I think Lois is fine." Strange question, but then Wendy could be a little odd. Meg put the large glass of Pinot on the bar in front of her.

"Well that's good. Have you been over to the exhibition yet? At the library?"

Meg remembered Wendy was in charge of the Viking stuff they'd found in the foundations up on Winthrop. She hadn't paid much attention to that whole fuss—she'd been so busy here. "I haven't yet, Wendy. But I promise I will soon."

"You'd better hurry because they're going off to Boston in three days." Wendy frowned. "Pretty sure that's the last we'll ever see of it. It's not right, you know. That find belongs to Provincetown."

In all honesty, looking at a bunch of Viking knives and jewellery wasn't really Meg's idea of a great time, but Wendy was so excited about it. "I promise I'll go day after tomorrow when I'm off. How's that?"

Wendy smiled and raised her glass to Meg. "Perfect. If you give me a time, I'll meet you down there and show you around."

Meg groaned inwardly. "I'll text you when I know my schedule, okay?"

"Okay, honey."

With Wendy appeased, Meg set about getting the bar ready to close down. It was still early, but the customers would start going home soon. If she could get everything done by closing, she'd have a shot at getting home before the sun came up—not that there was any sun to be had in Provincetown right now.

She paused at the table in the corner. Carl Winters always sat in the same place most nights when he had a few bucks. Meg knew he didn't have a place to live, and he'd always make his one drink last all night. Meg didn't mind. She let him stay just as long as he wanted. Better here in the warm than out there.

"Hey, Carl," she said, picking up his empty glass.

"Evening, Meg," he replied.

"This done?"

"Sure. I'll get out of your hair." He stood to leave, just as he did every time.

"You feel like sticking around? I was going to have a burger before I headed home and wouldn't mind some company," Meg said.

They did this most nights too. Meg was dog-tired and wanted nothing more than her bed, but at least she had a bed. From what she could tell, Carl had his car—which he slept in—and not much else.

"Oh, you must be beat, and I don't want to keep you," Carl said.

"You'd be doing me a favour. I have to toss the food tonight anyway. We'd stop it going to waste," Meg said, sticking to her part of the script.

"Well, if you're sure."

"Give me fifteen minutes to clear up, and I'll get the burgers on the grill," Meg said.

"Let me help you close up. Least I can do," Carl said.

Meg patted his shoulder. "That would be great, thanks." And tonight more than most nights, she meant it. She'd put the money for their food in the register tomorrow.

CHAPTER TWO

Lane stepped out of the terminal into the crisp morning air, and being this close to the ocean, it smelled clean and salty. Lane took in lungfuls of it. It definitely beat the stale, pressurized air on the two planes she'd had to take to get here.

Lane had called a cab from the tiny Provincetown airport. It was the strangest airport she'd ever been in. Literally one room with a vast collection of snow globes on the only counter in the place.

And the plane ride over here from Boston had been something else. Lane didn't consider herself a bad flyer, but that plane was small and loud and looked like it might drop out of the sky any minute and plummet to the earth in a fiery ball of regret and bad life choices.

Fortunately, the plane was in good condition, the pilot experienced and friendly, and so she was still alive.

She had managed to get a room in town thanks to a last-minute cancellation. She'd had no idea Provincetown was such a popular destination, though she had to admit that she hadn't researched it at all. She was here because Meg was. She'd get her back and head home to London with Meg. Or if Meg wanted to stay in the US, they'd find a way to do that.

Lane's attention was drawn to the sound of an engine. It

was coming closer and getting louder. Slightly alarmed, she wondered what on earth could make such a noise.

Then she saw it. It was painted all the colours of the rainbow and maybe even some that had never been seen before. The car was splattered in mud and was adorned with various bumper stickers saying things like *Fenway Forever*, *Two words, One finger*, and Lane's personal favourite *I don't like you*. The monstrosity did not look the slightest bit roadworthy. Lane squinted. Did the car really have a fluffy pink steering wheel?

The vehicle pulled up beside her, and the driver's window rolled down slowly. "Boyd?" a voice from inside asked.

She dragged her suitcase over. "Are you here for me?" Please God this wasn't her cab.

A woman in her late fifties stuck her head out the window and scowled at Lane. "I don't know. Are you Lane Boyd?"

"I am."

"Then yes, I'm here for you. Name's Cab, Dolores Cab." The woman rolled her window back up and stared straight ahead. There was a click, and the car's boot popped open. Lane guessed she wouldn't be getting any help with her bag from Dolores Cab.

She dumped it in the boot and climbed in the back seat. "I'm going to the Monument Bed and Breakfast. Do you know it?" Lane asked.

The woman stared at her in the rear-view mirror. "Yeah, I know it. Belt up."

With that, Dolores stuck the car into drive and tore out of the car park going what had to be well over the speed limit. Lane was thrown back against the seat. "You've lived here long?" Lane searched around for conversation as she tried to steady herself.

"You want to talk the whole way there? Because that'll cost extra," Dolores snapped.

Lane sighed and closed her eyes.

It took less than ten minutes to get to the bed and breakfast—which made sense because they drove there at about forty miles an hour. Dolores had not taken one turn she'd felt required her foot to leave the accelerator. Lane imagined there was a dent from where Dolores kept it permanently pressed to the floor.

Lane shot out of the cab, grabbed her bag, and just about managed to shut the boot before Dolores revved then roared out of the little car park, spraying Lane with gravel.

Lane shook her head.

"Oh, dear, you took Dolores Cab."

Lane spun round at the voice. "There was a card at the airport. I had no idea she would be deranged."

A woman stood on the doorstep of the Beacon looking like she wanted to laugh. "Dolores isn't dangerous, don't worry. Eccentric, perhaps."

"She's not at all friendly. Is she even licensed?" Lane dragged her suitcase up the small set of steps.

"In answer to both your questions, absolutely not," the woman said. "I'm Ella—I own the Beacon."

"Lane Boyd. You're English."

"I am. I moved here about ten years ago. Come inside— it's freezing this morning."

Lane followed Ella inside. "Is it always so overcast?"

"No, the weather's been particularly bad the last week or so. Tea? Coffee?" Ella asked.

"No, thank you. I'd just like to go to my room and recover from Dolores Cab." Lane grinned.

Ella laughed. "I don't blame you. When you are recovered,

there's tea and coffee in the kitchen. We put out bread and pastries for breakfast as well, so help yourself."

"Thank you."

Lane followed Ella up a narrow set of stairs to the first floor—wait, second floor. The place was nice. Homey. Not exactly what she was used to, but it was clean and central, and she didn't plan on staying long. Just long enough to get Meg back.

❖

Meg rolled over and opened her eyes. She silenced the alarm on her phone. It took her a minute to work out where she was. Home. Couch. Shit, she didn't even get to drink her tea, and the TV turned itself off hours ago. She sat up and shook out the crick in her neck. She really had to stop doing this. Her neck would ache all day and bring on a headache that aspirin wouldn't touch. Shit.

And why was she awake so early? Who set their alarm for eight a.m. when they only got home at three a.m.? Oh, right. Joanne. After the conversation with Wendy last night, Meg wanted to drop by and see if she needed anything. And to find out when she'd be back at work. Despite the extra money, the long hours were kicking Meg's ass.

She yawned wide enough to crack her jaw and went into the kitchen. Goddammit, no coffee. She'd forgotten to go to the store. Which meant she also had no bread for toast. She rifled around the cabinets hoping for something. Maybe a bagel she'd forgotten about, a spoonful of coffee at the bottom of a packet she'd pushed to the back of the shelf.

But no. Nothing. Meg didn't forget about food or open a new packet before the old one was finished. That behaviour was ingrained in her from a lifetime of being broke. She'd grown up poor, and because she'd spent so long saving for her dreams—the year in London, her own bar—she lived as frugally as possible. She rarely ate out or went to the movies unless it was on a date. And she hadn't been on a date in months.

Even in London she'd gotten most places on foot and made the most of the free museums and galleries. Well, until Lane. But Lane was generous—too generous sometimes, and it made Meg uncomfortable. Sure, Lane had a ton of family money, but Meg liked to pay her own way. She didn't want anyone saying she didn't. Another hangover from growing up poor, she guessed. Always feeling less than everyone else because they could afford stuff her mother couldn't. New sneakers, class trips, vacations.

Meg loved her mother and admired her. She'd brought up four kids by herself and worked two jobs. She'd never taken a handout in her life, and Meg respected that. Her mother was her hero. Speaking of which, she should call her later. Meg tried to remember the last time she'd spoken to her mother. Last week? The week before? The fact she couldn't remember wasn't good.

First things first, though. She needed to check in on Joanne and go to the store. And they were in opposite directions. And she had to be at work at eleven a.m. Maybe this one time she could treat herself to coffee and a muffin at the Wired Puppy. The hours she was working, she deserved a treat.

Meg jumped in the shower and cranked up the cold water to try to wake herself up.

❖

Lane took a left at the top of Winthrop Street like Ella told her. Construction machinery sat idly by. Lane remembered—

this was where they found that Viking crap. Maybe they'd been forced to stop work.

She had to hand it to Provincetown. It was a beautiful place. Like a lot of Brits, she'd grown up watching American films, and Provincetown was the epitome of what she thought a small New England town in America should look like. It was perfect. Most of the clapboard houses were freshly painted with bright coloured trim. Front gardens overflowed with flowers, and shop signs were hand painted and swung from chains above the doors.

Ella warned her the Wired Puppy did great coffee but was a fair old walk from the Beacon. Lane decided to see how far she got. From the looks of things, there were tons of places to have breakfast. Plus, she needed to wake herself up, and a walk would do her good even if the weather was miserable.

If she was honest with herself, Lane was also hoping to run into Meg. The town was small, so it wasn't totally out of the realm of possibility. And a chance meeting would be better than asking around about Meg like some kind of stalker.

When Meg dumped her, Lane deleted her number and all the messages between them. In hindsight, that had been a mistake because now she'd have to try and find her instead of just texting.

Lane only hoped that if she did run into her in the centre of town, Meg would be alone. Lane hadn't really thought about what she'd do if Meg had met someone new. Every time that particular little nugget popped into her brain, she booted it right back out again.

Lane tried not to think about the last time she saw Meg. She knew things weren't going great—Meg was distant and making more and more excuses not to see her. A small part of her had known that when Meg told her they needed to talk, it wouldn't be about anything good. Still, Meg actually saying the words had hit her in the gut and taken her breath away.

❖

"Can I get you a drink?" Lane asked. Meg had asked to meet her in a pub by the river near Meg's flat.

"No, I'll get them," Meg said.

They stood awkwardly at the bar together, not speaking. Lane knew something was up for sure now. On the way over, she'd half convinced herself it was nothing, that she was imagining it. But seeing Meg's unsmiling face and guarded eyes told Lane all she needed to know. She was about to get dumped.

Lane followed Meg to a table. "Is everything okay, Meg?" Lane knew it wasn't.

"We need to talk." Meg took a deep breath. She wouldn't meet Lane's eyes.

"Uh-oh. Nothing good ever followed those words." Lane tried to joke but her stomach was in knots.

"No, I guess not. Look, Lane—"

"Are you dumping me?"

Lane saw Meg wince, and she knew. Her heart beat hard in her chest, and her eyes prickled. Shit, this hurt.

"It's not about dumping you. I just don't think we're right for each other. We knew it was going to be a short-term thing—I'm heading back to the US next year. I just think it's better to end it now."

"Why?" Lane struggled to keep her voice from wobbling.

"We're so different." Meg reached for her hand, and Lane couldn't bring herself to pull it away. She wanted to. She wanted to make Meg hurt like she was hurting. To lash out and

share out some of the pain. She didn't, though. She hadn't been raised that way.

Lane kept her hand where it was. She let Meg take it and hold it and tried not to think this was the last time she'd touch her. She furiously blinked away tears that formed in the corners of her eyes and tried to speak around the knot in her throat.

"You never meant this to last?"

"I was only ever going to be here two years. But that's not the point. The point is that we're so different, Lane."

"We aren't so different," Lane replied.

"Maybe it doesn't seem like it now, but those little differences will get bigger. They'll destroy us," Meg said.

"Is this to do with your father? Him walking out? You're worried we'll end up like your parents."

When Meg recoiled, Lane realized her mistake. Meg never wanted to talk about anything even verging on her vulnerabilities. She couldn't handle the idea she wasn't invincible.

"It has nothing to do with that. I want to buy my own bar and build a career for myself. You want to party and spend your family's money." Meg let go of Lane's hand, and Lane left it there for a moment, hanging between them in an awkward disembodied way, before she picked up her drink.

"I see. Well, thanks for letting me know. You could have just ghosted me, but you didn't. I appreciate it." Lane channelled her mother. She was the coldest person Lane knew. Lane forced that same coldness into her voice and into her eyes.

"You're welcome." Meg looked confused.

"Is that all?" Lane stood.

"Yes, but—"

"Good luck, Meg. I hope you get your bar."

Lane refused to look back as she left the pub. The knot in her throat was growing, and the tears were coming too fast to blink away. All she had to do was get to the car. Just get to the car.

❖

Lane took a deep breath and shook off the memory. She saw a nice looking restaurant set back slightly from the road and decided to go in. Admittedly she'd only gotten about a hundred feet down Provincetown's main street, Commercial Street, but she was hungry. And she needed tea—or coffee—and she could look for Meg later. Her stomach growled in agreement.

Inside, the place had vinyl checked floors and bright red and chrome booths. There were windows all the way round and, at the back, views of the ocean.

A waitress showed Lane to her table and handed her a menu. "Coffee?" she asked.

"Yes, please," Lane said. And then, because she couldn't help herself, "Do you know a Meg Daltry?"

"Meg? Sure. She works over at the Squealing Pig."

"The Squealing what?" Lane put down her menu.

The waitress laughed. "The Squealing Pig. It's a bar about ten minutes' walk from here. Right down Commercial. You a friend of hers?"

"No, not really," Lane said.

The waitress frowned. "Not really? Guess I should have asked before I told you where she worked."

"No, no. I mean, I am a friend. I knew her in London. I'm here to surprise her." Lane fiddled with the salt shaker.

"You flew all the way from London to surprise her? You her girlfriend?"

"Yes—I mean, no. I used to be. We split up."

"Split up?"

"Broke up. Well, she dumped me."

The waitress's frown rearranged itself into something that looked like pity. "Oh, I get it. I'm sorry, that sucks. I got dumped too last week. But flying all the way over here…isn't that a little desperate?"

Lane died inside. This was not how she wanted things to go. Did she seem desperate? "I was hoping it would look more like, you know, a grand gesture. Like I'm serious about her."

"Sweetheart, if she dumped you, I'm not sure she wants you to be serious about her. I know Meg a little bit. She's all about work. About that bar in Boston she's going to open. I've never seen her with anyone since she got here. She doesn't strike me as the type for big romantic gestures. I'm going to get you that coffee now." The waitress patted Lane's hand before walking off.

Fuck. Fuck, fuck, fuckity fuck. Lane covered her face with her hands. It hadn't occurred to her that Meg dumped her because she wasn't interested in a relationship—or rather she'd chosen not to think about that. Lane had decided it was because Meg didn't see a future with her. She hadn't allowed herself to consider the possibility it might be because Meg just really wasn't that into her. And now she'd flown thousands of miles across the ocean and made a fool out of herself in front of the waitress.

"Excuse me," she called to the waitress who was making her way back over with coffee. "Is there anywhere around here that sells art supplies?"

The waitress frowned again. "You're going to paint her a picture?"

"What? No. No, not at all."

"Further up there's a store on the left. About five minutes' walk. They don't open until ten, though."

Ten would be fine. Lane decided she'd have her coffee, but she wasn't hungry at all any more. Painting helped her think. Helped her sort out her feelings. Meg once told her she should try to sell them, that she was really good, but Lane knew Meg was just being kind. She painted as a hobby and nothing more. There was a time she thought she might like to be an artist, but as her parents said, how likely was it that she would ever make a career out of that?

Lane drank her coffee and tried not to think about how coming here might have been a huge mistake.

Chapter Three

 Outer Cape Echo
1 hour ago

LOCAL WOMAN BITES GUEST: Last week cops were called to a local woman's bed and breakfast after she bit a customer for complaining about the cold coffee at breakfast. The local woman, who cannot be named for legal reasons, apparently latched on to the guest's shoulder and bit down after he told her the coffee had gone cold. "It was the craziest thing. All I asked was could we get some warm coffee, and she came at me like a rabid dog." The guest from Florida continued, "It's no way to treat a paying customer. She won't be getting a good review from me."

The woman was arrested at the scene and later released on bail.

---

418 Likes   *7 Comments*

Patty Wold: My nephew got bit by a kid at school just yesterday. And I heard someone down the street got bit by their husband. Maybe there's some biting disease going around?

Dolores Cab: Idiot. Patty, the only disease going around is stupid and I'm pretty sure you have it. Not your fault, you caught it from your parents.

Molly Price: I think there's something going around too. My cousin got bit by one of her customers when she was doing her hair this morning. Why isn't anyone looking into this? I think we need some help in Provincetown.

Dolores Cab: Why don't you quit whining, Molly? Might not help you, but we'd sure feel better. Failing that, I hear putting your head in boiling tar is a definite cure to this biting disease.

Molly Price: Stop trolling me, Dolores. I will report you.

Moderator: *Dolores Cab*. Do we have to put you in another time out?

Dolores Cab: *[deleted by poster]*

❖

Lane tried not to think about her conversation with the waitress. She concentrated on putting one foot in front of the other and making it to the art supply shop. She would buy things, go to the beach, and paint. Once she started painting, everything would become clearer. She'd be calm. It was always like that when she painted.

Lane was so focused on getting to the art shop she almost walked straight into a little girl.

"Shit, sorry." She cringed at the swear word. She wasn't used to kids. "Sorry, I didn't mean to swear. Please don't repeat that word—it's not nice."

Then she really looked at the kid. She was young. Much too young to be out by herself. Lane crouched down in front of her. "Hi. My name is Lane. What's yours?"

"Lois."

The little girl still had to look up to meet Lane's eyes. "Where's your mummy, Lois? Or your daddy?"

"My mommy is sick. You talk funny."

Lane smiled. "I'm from England. Does your mummy know you're out by yourself?"

Lois shook her head. "I have to go to school. I'm late."

"How old are you?"

"I'll be seven in December."

"So you're six?"

"No. I'm seven in December." Lois's little brow furrowed.

"But that means you're six now," Lane said. Why was she arguing with a child?

"But *I am seven in December.*" Lois enunciated each word as though she was speaking to someone very slow.

"Okay, fine. But the point is you probably aren't allowed out by yourself."

"I don't want to be late for school. Mrs. Shaw will be mad. Excuse me, I need to go now." Lois started to walk off.

Lane gently took her shoulders to stop her leaving. "Lois, I think we should take you back home to your mum. She's going to be worried. And you really shouldn't be wandering about by yourself." Or talking to strangers. But she figured she shouldn't mention that right now.

"I'm not wandering by myself, I'm going to school."

"Who usually takes you to school?"

"Mommy."

"But she's sick?"

Lois nodded.

"Then we should take you home and maybe your mum can call someone to take you."

"But I'll be late." Lois crossed her little arms.

This was unravelling. Lane just wanted to get her art stuff

and go to the beach. "I know. Mrs. Shaw will understand. Your mum can tell her it's not your fault."

"Then she won't be mad?"

"No, she won't be mad. Well, maybe she'll be mad at your mum."

"I don't want her to be mad at my mom."

"Your mum can handle it—don't worry. Shall we go?" Lane stood and held out her hand. Lois seemed to consider the possibilities for a second, and then, to Lane's relief, took her hand.

"Okay, but you have to tell Mrs. Shaw why I'm late. Then she can be mad at you."

"Fine. Where do you live?"

Lois pointed to a side street.

"Just down there?"

"Uh-huh."

"Let's go then."

Lane briefly wondered if Lois was a ploy for muggers. Lead her down a dark alley and rob her. No, she was just being paranoid. But it was dark down there. The whole sky was dark, in fact, like an early winter evening. It was strange.

Meg knocked on Joanne's front door. After a minute, she heard footsteps coming down the hall, and then the door opened.

For a second, Meg couldn't breathe. She blinked. Blinked again. She tried to get her throat to work.

"Lane."

For her part, Lane looked equally stunned. "Meg."

"What are you doing here?" The last place Meg expected

to find Lane Boyd was at Joanne's house. Her being in Provincetown was weird enough, but at Joanne's?

"I found her daughter wandering around outside. I brought her home. I…Wow, this is not how I wanted you to find out I was here."

What did that mean? Lane came to Provincetown to see her? Or she was here and knew Meg was and didn't want her to find out from someone else? What the hell was going on?

"I'm sorry, you've got me at a disadvantage," Meg said.

"I know. I know I have. Look, can we talk? Not here. But later. Joanne is really ill. I think she needs a doctor, but she won't let me call one."

Meg pushed past Lane and tried to ignore how her belly tightened as she brushed against her. Lane was still hot.

"Let me see her."

Meg almost gagged at the smell in Joanne's bedroom. It was sweet and rotten—like fruit gone off. "Joanne?"

Joanne lay beneath the covers unmoving. "Joanne? It's Meg." Meg took a few steps further inside the room and tried not to throw up. The only explanation Meg could think of for that smell was a festering wound or something equally gross. "Joanne, honey, I'm going to call an ambulance. I think that cut you got is infected."

Joanne rolled over and blinked up at Meg. "I told that other woman I'm okay. Just sick. I have a really bad cold."

"I think it's more than that. I wish you'd let us call you a doctor," Lane said. She moved up right behind Meg, and Meg could feel her warmth. "You smell awful."

"Lane!" Meg said.

"What? It smells like something went off in here. I'm sorry, Joanne, but it does. And Lois was wandering about by herself outside. I really think you need a doctor. Probably a hospital."

"Okay, okay. I'll call a doctor. I think you're right. I'm sorry about Lois. I'll get my sister to take her." Joanne struggled into a sitting position. She really did look terrible.

"You want us to do it?" Meg asked.

"No, no, you've both done enough. I should get up and air this place out anyway. I think I left something out in the kitchen. I think that's the smell. I promise—I'll call a doctor."

Meg wasn't convinced the smell was coming from the kitchen, but she didn't know Joanne that well, and she didn't want to push. "Okay, listen, we'll go. I'm going to drop by later to see how you are, though. Call if you need anything."

"I will. I promise. Thank you," Joanne said. "And I'll call my sister right now."

❖

Meg dragged in deep lungfuls of air once they were back outside. Lane was doing the same beside her. She felt uneasy about leaving Joanne, but what could she do? Joanne wouldn't let her call a doctor or an ambulance. She'd check back later, and if Joanne was the same, she would call regardless of what Joanne wanted.

Right now, she had to deal with the other issue in front of her. Lane.

"So, you're in Provincetown," Meg said, pathetically stating the obvious.

"Yeah." Lane kicked at a loose stone.

"Why?" Meg watched as Lane looked off somewhere past her shoulder and took a deep breath.

"For you. I came for you."

"Why?" Meg blurted out and then regretted it when she saw Lane wince.

"Look, can we go for a walk? Talk?" Lane asked.

"I can't. I have to be at work soon."

"Later, then? When you've finished?" Lane said.

"I don't finish until after one a.m. We're short-staffed," Meg said, painfully aware of how weak that sounded. Lane had come all the way from London for her, so the least she could do was hear her out. In all honesty, she was floored. She didn't think Lane had been that bothered about their break-up—if you could even call it that. They'd never really been together in the first place.

"Fine." Lane nodded and sighed. "Is there any day this week when you might be free?"

"What for, Lane? What is this about? Are you seriously telling me you came all the way from London to get me back? We weren't even together, not really. It was a holiday romance. Fun. Nothing more."

Lane looked at her then, dead in the eyes, and Meg could see she'd hurt her. "It was more than that for me. I...I mean I think I'm—"

"No. Don't say it, Lane. Jesus. Look, I have to go to work. You still have the same cell number?"

Lane nodded.

"I'll call you. I will. Just...I need to get to work."

Before Lane could answer, Meg pushed past her and almost ran out of the alley. This was beyond crazy. Never in a million years would she have thought Lane would come all the way from London for her. It was the last thing Meg wanted. Even though part of her thrilled at the idea. She was just flattered, though, right? It wasn't anything more than that. It couldn't be. She didn't have time for sleep, let alone a relationship. And certainly not one with Lane.

Lane was childish and aimless and selfish. But she was sweet and funny and generous too. And hot. Meg had forgotten how hot she was. Damn it, it was just hormones and flattery and she had to get to work, and she most definitely didn't have time to think about Lane and how she'd almost told Meg she loved her.

❖

Well, that went just about as badly as Lane could have imagined. Meg wouldn't even meet with her to talk—don't call me, I'll call you. Add to that the fact Lane tried to tell Meg she loved her, and Meg wouldn't even let her say it. She didn't need to when the look of horror on Meg's face said it all. Lane was humiliated. Utterly humiliated.

What would she do now? She'd only come here for Meg, and it was quite clear Meg didn't want her. The waitress was right. Lane looked desperate. Pathetic. And it was too early for a drink. Fucking hell.

Lane walked aimlessly down Commercial. Shops were just starting to open, though the streets were still quiet. She felt empty and crushed and so, so foolish. She wanted to go home, but a bigger part of her wanted to stay. To convince Meg to give her a chance. And that was even more pathetic. Meg had been very clear. She did not want Lane, so why did a small part of Lane still hold out hope?

Lane found herself standing outside a place called Whalers Wharf. It seemed to be a small shopping arcade. There were boards out the front advertising shops inside. One was for tarot, or psychic mumbo jumbo, to use its proper title. But Lane had nothing else to do, and who knew? Maybe the tarot reader would have some answers for her.

She walked down a short hall with shops lining either side. The building was open at the back with a view of the sea. Lane hesitated for a moment, still unsure about whether to go through with the tarot reading. She stepped outside and leaned against the railings.

Lane felt strange, discombobulated and slightly hopeless. She sighed. The sea was rough and grey and reflected her mood. Lane glanced to the left and squinted. In the distance she could see a sand dune, which should be underwater at this time of day. There was a man on it. Or at least she thought it was a man. He was tall and blueish in tone. Weird. On second thoughts, it couldn't be a person. Not out there. Not in this weather. It was probably a buoy or a rock. Sometimes your mind played tricks on you and made things look like something else. Lane turned and walked back inside.

Alice didn't look like a tarot reader. She was in her late thirties and had short brown ringlets. With her bright red floral print dress, chunky jewellery, and carefully manicured red nails she looked more like a sexy fifties housewife. She also wore a key around her neck, which intrigued Lane.

"Come in and sit down."

Lane did as she was told. Alice's shop was really just a small room, one flight up, by the balcony. Inside were two chairs and a low table. There was a door at the back which Lane guessed went to a bathroom and maybe an office.

"You're lucky you caught me. I'm heading out of town for a couple weeks today. I nearly didn't open the store," Alice said.

Lane wasn't sure how to respond. "I suppose it's fate?"

Alice laughed and it lit her face. "Or I had way too much red wine last night and decided not to drive until this afternoon."

Lane smiled. "Yeah, or that. So, what's the key around your neck? Some kind of tarot talisman?"

Alice laughed. "Not at all. It's a key to the bathrooms on

the first floor. All the store owners have them. They used to be open to the public, but they aren't in great shape. Instead of fixing them, they shut them off. Now only store owners can use them."

Lane felt a bit silly. Key to a toilet. "I see. Sorry, I just thought…never mind."

"Don't worry about it. So, do you have a question in mind? For the cards?" Alice sat opposite Lane and picked up a deck of cards from the table.

"I don't know. I mean, I haven't done this before."

"That's okay. May I ask what brought you here today?" Alice asked.

Lane sighed deeply. "Well, there's this woman."

"Oh, honey, there always is," Alice said.

Something about Alice's tone made Lane laugh. "Fuck, I'm pathetic, aren't I?" Lane buried her head in her hands.

"Not at all." Alice tapped Lane's hands, and she took them away from her face. "If it's not a woman, then it's careers, kids, finances. We like to think we're unique, but really, we're all basically the same. Same hopes, same fears, same dreams."

"Yeah?" Lane asked. Alice's words made her feel a little less alone.

"Truly. So tell me about this woman." Alice sat back in her chair.

"Don't I need to shuffle the cards or something first?" Lane asked.

"We'll get to that. First, tell me about the woman."

❖

Meg used her ass to close the front door. She had two heavy bags of shopping in each hand, and she was dead on her feet. Lane had texted earlier to say she was on her way over to Meg's place. She'd promised to cook and tidy up, but Meg wasn't counting on it. Lane had offered before, and when Meg got home, Lane had been sitting on the sofa with cans of soda and open bags of chips scattered around her.

Meg didn't smell dinner this time either and guessed it would be the same situation—Lane camped out on the couch with an apologetic smile on her face. Meg braced herself.

"Hey, babe. Is that you?" Lane called out.

"Yep." Meg walked into the living room. Just as she thought.

"Sorry, I didn't get round to dinner. I thought we could go out. My treat. We can grab some food and maybe a few drinks in town. What do you think?" Lane said without looking away from the TV.

Meg could feel the frustration bubbling up inside her. The place was a mess. She'd just worked a twelve-hour shift. She'd given Lane a key to her place, and now she bitterly regretted it. Who gave someone they were casually dating a key, anyway? Someone who was getting into a relationship, that's who. Something she had been avoiding for years. And now she knew why.

"Not tonight. I'm tired. I went shopping, so I'll cook," Meg said and tried to keep her temper. She reminded herself that this was Lane.

"Come on. It'll be fun." Lane tilted her head back and pursed her lips for a kiss.

"No, Lane. I'm tired. I've done a long shift, and I want to sit on the couch for half an hour then go to bed."

Lane turned fully on the couch. "Okay. I'll get takeaway. What do you fancy?"

"I don't want takeaway. It's expensive, and there's food in the house." Meg kicked off her shoes, rounded the couch, and started picking up the crap Lane had left scattered about.

"Leave it—I'll tidy up."

"You will? You were supposed to tidy up before, but I can see a pile of dirty washing from here that's mostly yours anyway. You were supposed to cook, but instead you've set up camp on the couch and made even more mess." Meg picked up a T-shirt. "Why do you have so much stuff here anyway?"

When had Lane pretty much moved in? And why hadn't Meg noticed before? Well, she was noticing now. It was her mom and dad all over again before he walked out on them.

"Shit, I'm sorry. I know I said I would, but I got sidetracked." Lane laughed.

Meg lost it. "From what? You don't work. Don't do much of anything, from what I can tell. You certainly don't clean up after yourself. Jesus, Lane. This was supposed to be fun, but it's not fun any more. It's hard work. You're hard work."

"Because you're always at work. You're always too tired to do anything." Lane jumped up off the couch. "Let's go out. Call in sick tomorrow or something."

Meg's anger died. This was how it would be, she realized. Lane was a child. It wasn't her fault exactly. She was offering Meg the same kind of life—Lane could easily afford to support them both on her allowance. But this was how it would always be between them. Meg being the sensible one. Meg cleaning up. Meg making sure there was food in the house. Lane was immature and didn't want to change. Meg didn't blame her. She wasn't a bad person at all—she was wonderful, in fact—if you wanted that life too. And Meg didn't. She wanted something she'd built with her own hard work. Something she could be proud of.

Meg realized it was over. Whatever it was she and Lane were doing wasn't working, and it had to stop. It had already gone much further than she intended.

Meg sighed. Lane was looking at her like a puppy that

knew it had done something wrong but wasn't sure what. And that summed up their relationship. This thing needed to end.

❖

Meg let herself into the Squealing Pig and was surprised to find it empty. Usually Callie, their cook, was already at work and getting ready for the day. But the place was dark, made darker still by the strange weather, and the normal sounds of clanging and cursing from the kitchen were absent.

Meg had a sinking feeling in her stomach. She checked the machine and saw a dreaded red blinking light. She hit play, and sure enough, there was a message from Callie telling Meg she wouldn't be in today. In fairness, she sounded pretty terrible on her voicemail. But that didn't help Meg. She'd have to call Fran, the owner. There was no way Meg could run the bar and the kitchen by herself. It also meant another late finish. Callie was going away to college in the fall, and she sometimes worked extra shifts behind the bar after the night cook came on.

Meg had been hoping Callie would cover for her tonight. She'd handled the whole Lane thing terribly. On the way over, she'd decided to meet up with Lane and talk things over. She'd flown all the way over here and Meg owed her something. She couldn't give Lane what she came for, but that didn't mean she had to be obnoxious about it.

It didn't look like that was going to happen, though. Meg sighed and rubbed her eyes. There weren't enough hours in the damn day. She still wanted to go over to Joanne's to check on her. And she remembered she'd promised Wendy she'd go see the exhibition in the library too. On her day off. It was the last thing she wanted to do, but Wendy was so excited about it, and she was a good customer. Actually, that could work out well.

Maybe she could invite Lane to the exhibition, and they could go for a coffee and talk after.

Meg decided to text Lane. She was pretty sure she'd kept her number after they broke up. But if not, it wouldn't be too hard to find out where she was staying and get a message to her there.

Meg picked up her cell phone and started making calls.

CHAPTER FOUR

A lice turned over the first tarot card. It showed a blind-folded and bound woman surrounded by swords.

"Well, that can't be good," Lane said.

"It's the eight of swords. It represents frustration and obstacles—constraint. Something's been holding you back. You've been going down dead ends for a long time."

Lane stayed silent. The truth of Alice's words hit her straight in the gut.

"But this placement means that's coming to an end," Alice continued. "Recently you've taken control of your own destiny. Your luck is changing, Lane."

Lane cleared her throat. "The decision it's talking about. Is that coming here? To Provincetown?"

"I can't tell you that. But if you think it's that, then it probably is," Alice said before turning over another card. "Okay, now this one's interesting."

Lane leaned forward and looked at the card. A skeleton in armour holding a black flag and riding a horse. Great. "How's that interesting? Obviously, it's saying it's curtains for me."

"What?" Alice looked confused.

"I'm going to die." Lane tapped the card with one finger. "It's death, right?"

"No, honey, you aren't going to die. None of these cards

should be taken literally. The death card can mean a lot of things. Rarely the death of a person. More like an ending is coming. That kind of thing."

"What's ending for me?" Lane asked.

Alice frowned. "Something is coming. Something big. It'll come on you suddenly, and it'll mean the end of things as they are."

"I'm not convinced that's good, Alice."

"Lane, moving forward means other things have to fall away—or die. You can't move on otherwise. This event could be anything, maybe something good." Except Alice's frown wasn't reassuring Lane it *was* good.

"Okay, fine. Look, thanks for the reading. How much do I owe you?"

"I haven't finished yet," Alice said. She turned over another card, and Lane saw her blanch. That was not good at all. Lane refused to look at the card. If she didn't look, then it wasn't there.

"I think I've heard enough." Lane stood up, and her chair toppled over. She hastily handed Alice some bills and headed for the door.

"Wait," Alice called after her. Lane stopped, turned.

"Take this. It may help you. I don't know why, but you have to take it." Alice held out a card face down. When Lane made no move to take it, Alice shoved it in her hand. Lane stuffed it in her jeans pocket without looking at it and hurried out with the card burning hot against her.

Lane could feel her chest tighten and her breathing shorten. She had the overwhelming urge to run, to get outside. So she did.

She took the stairs two at a time and threw open the doors on the ground floor. Bent over double, she tried to catch her breath. Panic attack. That's what it was. She hadn't had one of those in a while. Shakily, Lane wiped the back of her hand across her forehead. She was sweating, and her hair was damp.

Fucking hell. Lane stood upright, feeling better now, and took in deep breaths of fresh sea air. Her head cleared, and she felt more herself. What was all that about? Why had she had a total meltdown over a tarot reading? She didn't even believe in that shit. It was the skeleton on the horse. Death. Lane's gut quivered as she remembered the picture on the card. It had creeped her out, that was all. Stupid. She'd had a shitty day, and that stupid tarot reading had compounded it.

Except Alice was lovely. And the reading was fine—good, even. Up until that death card. But even that hadn't exactly been *bad*. So what was wrong with her then?

Lane's mobile phone buzzed in her pocket.

She took it out. The battery was flashing red. She never remembered to charge the bloody thing. A message from Meg.

Full of hope and swooping feelings, Lane opened the message.

Hi. It's Meg. I behaved badly today. Can we meet tomorrow and talk?

The message was brief—very Meg—but Lane was filled with unreasonable hope anyway. She cautioned herself not to get excited. Meg wanted to talk, not get back together. But if she wanted to talk, then there was hope she could be convinced to listen to Lane, to hear her out. Lane started to tap out her reply, then stopped.

She shouldn't reply straight away, should she? It would look desperate. Maybe like she'd been sitting staring at her phone. She should wait. Give it a few minutes. Maybe a few hours? But not too long, or it would look contrived. Like she was trying *not* to reply too soon.

Shit. Lane hated this. There was a time when she'd loved the chase. Not any more and not with Meg. Lane just wanted her back.

She sighed and tucked the phone away. She'd go back to the B and B and reply then.

Lane kicked off her shoes and lay on the bed. It was comfortable, and the bed linen not half bad. She reread Meg's message. She wanted to meet tomorrow. Go for coffee. It was certainly something. It didn't mean anything, exactly, but it was a start, something to hold on to, to build on.

She was aware how desperate that made her, but she didn't care. She'd already fucked up with Meg once—well, twice really. Lane berated herself every day for just taking Meg's dumping her like it didn't matter. Maybe if she'd shown some fight in the first place, things would have turned out differently.

But she hadn't fought. She'd sat there and accepted it. By the time she'd gotten the guts to fight for Meg, she'd left. Gone, back to the US. No forwarding address, no goodbye. Lane only found out where she'd gone by chance. Three weeks ago she'd run into Meg's old boss at a club. She'd mentioned Meg was working in a bar in Provincetown because Meg's new boss had requested a reference from her.

Now, here Lane was. And she was waiting passively again. First, by running into Meg by chance and not going straight to find her. And now, by waiting for Meg to contact her about meeting. How would Meg know she'd changed if she just sat back like she'd always done and let others make the decisions for her. No. Lane would go to Meg's bar and talk to her there. Tonight.

❖

Meg looked up from where she was loading the dishwasher, and her stomach did that annoying swooping thing. Lane grinned at her and came up to the bar.

"How's it going?" she asked Meg.

"Busy. You?" Meg lifted a tray of glasses onto the dishwasher.

Lane shrugged. "I got your text. You wanted to talk?"

"Yeah, but not right now. I'm kind of up to my eyes in it. I thought I said tomorrow." Meg blew a strand of hair off her face. The night cook agreed to come in early, thank God, but her boss wasn't answering her phone, so Meg was on her own behind the bar. She'd been rushed off her feet and her temper was fraying. She tried not to be mad at Lane for turning up unannounced. It was a bar after all, and Lane could go where she liked.

"Can I give you a hand?" Lane asked, ignoring Meg's comment.

"No, that's all right. You want a drink?"

"I don't mind helping. Helped you enough back in London. Remember?"

Meg did remember. Lane made a habit of showing up near the end of her shift. A few times it had been busy, and Lane jumped behind the bar to help her out. Meg remembered being surprised that Lane actually knew what she was doing. And more than once she'd ended up helping Meg with a lot more than serving drinks.

"There we go, last one out the door," Lane said from behind her as she threw the bolts across the door.

"Thank God, I'm beat," Meg replied.

"How beat? Too beat?"

Meg turned and grinned. "Oh, never too beat for that."

"Excellent news," Lane said, and Meg's stomach

contracted as Lane leaned her elbows on the bar and looked Meg up and down. Meg loved it when Lane did that.

"You want to go home?" Meg asked and walked over to the bar.

Lane shook her head. "No, too far."

"You want to do it right here in the bar?" Meg pretended to be shocked.

"Why not?" Lane grinned.

"Lane Boyd. Are you suggesting we have sex right here in my place of work where anyone could walk in?" Meg tried not to laugh. She'd had no idea she was playful until she met Lane.

"That's exactly what I'm suggesting. Besides, the doors are locked. Everyone has gone home."

"Someone could come back."

"They'll get an eyeful then, won't they?" Lane said and leaped over the bar, making Meg squeal.

"No." She backed away from Lane, who advanced on her. "I'm serious. Stay away." She wasn't serious at all, and she knew Lane knew it.

"Or what?" Lane kept advancing.

"I'll call the cops." Meg was laughing now. She couldn't help it.

"I'll be finished by the time they get here," Lane said and pulled Meg into her arms.

"Lane Boyd, the great lover." Meg rolled her eyes. Lane was actually incredible in bed, but they had a standing joke she was terrible.

"You've never complained before," Lane said.

"You're finished before I can," Meg replied. "No, Lane!"

Suddenly, Meg was pulled off her feet and carried to the bar where Lane dropped her unceremoniously back onto her feet.

Meg leaned into Lane to keep her balance, and Lane used

the opportunity to kiss her hard on the lips. God, Meg loved to kiss her.

Meg pulled away from the kiss. "I've been thinking."

"No. Thinking bad, kissing good," Lane replied and went in for another one.

Meg put her hand over Lane's mouth to halt her progress. "You'll like this."

Lane raised her eyebrows.

Meg leaned in close and whispered in her ear, "Why don't you let me show you how it's done?"

Meg felt Lane flinch, then nod. Meg moved her hand from Lane's mouth and unbuttoned her jeans. She pulled them down to Lane's knees and dipped her thumbs just inside Lane's underwear, stroking, before she pulled those down too.

"Shit, Meg."

"Shh." Meg tilted her head and nipped Lane's earlobe. "Just watch."

Meg reached between Lane's legs and ran a finger along the place where her lips parted. God, Lane was wet. For her. The thought of that turned Meg on even more.

Meg got onto her knees and pulled Lane's clothing all the way off. She used her thumbs to part Lane again and breathed her in.

Lane groaned above her. She felt Lane's hands take hold of her hair and grip on tight. "Please, Meg."

Meg obliged, and her first taste of Lane was just as delicious as it always was. Meg used her tongue to circle Lane's clit slowly and without much pressure.

"Such a tease," Lane said, and Meg could hear the smile in her voice. She didn't answer.

Instead, Meg began to lick up and down, applying a little more pressure but not too much. She wanted Lane squirming under her mouth before she'd give her what she needed.

Meg felt Lane plant her legs wider, and then Lane's grip on her head tightened and pulled her in. So Meg stopped. She looked up. "You aren't in charge right now, baby. Remember?"

Lane laughed and rolled her eyes. "I forgot. Fine, I'll let you go at your own pace. But please, don't torture me for too much longer."

"Oh, I'm going to torture you a lot longer. It'll be good for you to wait for something you want, for once."

Lane laughed. "You're evil."

"You love it."

Meg got back to work. Despite what she'd said, she wouldn't make Lane wait. Meg put more pressure on Lane's clit and pushed one finger inside her. She flattened her tongue so she covered more of Lane's clit and made her strokes harder and faster. Meg could hear Lane's breathing quicken and feel her legs start to shake. Lane was going to come. Meg loved this part.

With a groan, Lane pushed herself hard into Meg's mouth and gripped her hair. She rode Meg's face so that Meg was buried in her. Lane coated her mouth and her nose, and Meg couldn't get enough. She carried on licking Lane until Lane pulled away, breathing heavily.

"Shit," Lane croaked.

Meg grinned and looked up. For a moment, her breath caught. Lane had a satisfied look in her eyes and a lazy smile on her lips, and Meg loved the idea she'd been the one to put them there. Lane was the most beautiful woman Meg had ever seen.

Kneeling there on the ground, staring up at Lane, Meg felt something inside her soften and crumble just a little. Then, on the heels of it, a swift surge of panic had her jumping back to her feet.

Meg took Lane's face in her hands and kissed her hard. Keep this purely about the sex, *she told herself.* Don't get attached, you can't afford to.

"Now I've given you a demonstration," Meg said, "I think it's time you showed me what you learned."

Lane laughed and spun her round. "Fair's fair," she said.

Lane's hand on her arm jolted Meg back to the present.

"Meg? I'm happy to help you behind the bar. I worked in that bar in Spain, so you know I know what I'm doing," Lane said.

Meg pushed the past out of her head. She definitely didn't need to be thinking about Lane like *that* right now. She was tired, and the bar was busy. Damn it, she was desperate. And she needed to pee. "Okay, that would be great. Thank you."

Lane came around the bar, and Meg watched her. Her stomach flipped, and that pissed her off. Meg knew she could easily fall into bed with Lane again—the sex had always been incredible. But she also knew that right now, Lane was weirdly vulnerable. She'd gotten some kind of crazy idea in her head about coming here and winning Meg back, as though she'd had her in the first place. Sex with Lane had trouble written all over it. Plus, Meg couldn't do that to her. Not when Lane obviously wanted so much more than Meg could give her.

"Okay, you can't operate the register because you don't have a login. Could you just help me take orders and I'll do the rest?" Meg asked.

"Of course." Lane smiled, and Meg wanted to lie down behind the bar and pull Lane on top of her. Not a good idea. And they were going to have to spend the next few hours rubbing up against each other. Great.

But some matters were urgent. "I need to go to the

bathroom. Could you just start making drinks, and I'll put them through when I get back? Most of these guys are on tabs anyway," Meg said.

"No problem." Lane turned away and started speaking to a customer.

Meg felt like she was taking advantage of Lane. It was clear Lane was helping her as part of her efforts to get Meg to go out with her again. But Meg couldn't run the bar by herself. She needed the help, and Lane was willing. After they closed, she'd talk to her. She'd be gentle but firm. She'd offer Lane friendship but nothing more. It was the best she could do.

❖

Lane enjoyed herself. She'd always been good behind the bar. Back when she'd spent those ten months in Spain, she'd had a lot of fun working at the hotel. She had good chat, and people liked her. It was no different here. But bar work was hard work, and Lane had eventually tired of it. Her family's money meant she didn't need to get a job if she didn't want to. Her parents had finally given up trying to convince her to follow her brother and sister into banking. The only thing she'd ever really loved was art, and it seemed her parents would rather she didn't work at all than become an artist.

Her aunt had been an artist and gotten in a scandal decades ago that was still talked about today. Lane couldn't remember the ins and outs, but she knew it involved several politicians, a paintbrush, and a call girl.

Her parents were terrified that if Lane became an artist too, the whole sordid chain of events would be rehashed and kicked off again in the newspapers and amongst their social circle.

Lane poured a beer and called out to Meg to ring it up. They worked well together—they always had. One always knew where the other was, so they never bumped into each other, even behind that tight bar back in London.

"It's slowing down now," Meg said using a tea towel to wipe her hands.

"Yeah, it got manic there for a while," Lane said.

"It's often busier than that, but a lot of people are out with the flu. I can't even get my boss on the phone. I guess she's sick too."

"Probably this weather. Not enough vitamin D or something," Lane said.

"Yeah, it's pretty bad for this time of year. Kind of like winter."

Lane nodded and struggled for something else to say. She couldn't think of anything.

"Can you hang around after we close up? I think we need to talk," Meg said.

Lane's heart leaped despite cautioning herself not to get excited. "Of course. I'd like that."

"Okay," Meg said.

They stood awkwardly for a moment longer, neither knowing what to say. They were saved by a customer signalling for another drink.

Meg locked the door and sighed. Her feet throbbed, and her head ached, but she half wished it wasn't closing time. Because that meant she'd have to talk to Lane. She'd have to let her down, and Meg hated to let anyone down. She'd seen the look in Lane's eyes when she asked her to stay behind so they could talk. Hope. She wasn't a stranger to it herself.

In her younger days, Meg had fallen in lust a few times with people who didn't reciprocate. On one occasion she'd been on the end of a talk herself, and it wasn't pleasant.

It wasn't that she wasn't attracted to Lane—hell, Lane was gorgeous. Tall, dark, and handsome. She was funny and sweet, and Meg knew she had a good heart. But Lane was aimless. She could be childish, and during their relationship—if you could call it that—Meg had increasingly begun to feel like her mother. Lane was an incredible artist, but she listened to her family too much and didn't seem to have the backbone to tell them to back off.

Lane could easily make it as an artist. She might never be rich, but she could make money at it, could support herself with her art. Of course, Meg wasn't exactly an expert in art, but she'd showed a friend who was an expert. Mia had loved Lane's work and said Lane could earn a living as a working artist. But Lane didn't want to know.

For some strange reason, Lane's family were totally against it. Basically told Lane they would never support that choice. Something to do with a scandal back in the day with one of Lane's relatives who'd been an artist. Whatever it was, Lane's family were dead against it. Meg supposed that would mean turning away from their money too, and she guessed that would be a hard thing for Lane—or anyone—to do.

It didn't matter anyway. Meg was never going to give Lane what she wanted. She worked too much to give anyone what they needed. Hell, if she couldn't even find time to call her own mother more than once every couple weeks, how would she sustain a relationship? Besides, she was focussed on the bar. It had been her dream for as long as she could remember, and she wasn't giving it up for anyone.

Meg's mother had given up her dreams for Meg's father.

And look where that got her. Debt up to her eyeballs and two kids to raise alone. There was no way Meg was going to fall into the same trap set by another bone-idle charmer like her dad had been. Not that Lane was like her father, exactly, but there was enough similarity there to make Meg think twice. Not that it ever took much to put Meg off a woman. She wasn't that deluded she didn't know a lot of it had more to do with her than with the woman. For as long as she could remember, she would look for a way out of a relationship as soon as she got in one.

Maybe she was afraid of losing her independence, or maybe she was so afraid of being in the same situation her mother had been that she was scarred for life.

Fabulous.

Behind her, Lane cleared her throat, and Meg realized she'd been standing at the door forever.

"Sorry, Lane. I guess I must have spaced out." She turned and walked back to the bar where Lane waited.

"Don't worry. It's been a long shift for you."

Then Lane gave Meg one of her heartbreaking smiles. It was vulnerable and cheeky at the same time—and so much better than the contrived ones Lane thought people liked. Shit, this was going to be hard.

"You want a drink?" Meg asked.

"If you're having one, I will," Lane said.

"Let's both have one. You still like vodka?" Meg set about getting glasses.

"I'll do it. You sit down and put your feet up. You've worked hard today." Lane came around the bar and took the glasses from Meg.

"Thanks. Make mine a large gin and tonic." Meg sat at the bar facing Lane, as though she was a customer.

"I wasn't very nice to you this morning, and I'm sorry," Meg said.

"That's okay—it must have been a shock to see me." Lane handed Meg her drink and leaned against the bar.

"That's not an excuse, but thank you for being gracious." Meg sipped her drink, buying time for what she was about to say next. "You know, when I texted you, I didn't expect you to come straight over. I was going to invite you to the Viking exhibition at the library."

Lane looked confused. "Why? Are you especially into Vikings?"

Meg laughed. "Not at all. I promised Wendy—our local historian—I'd go. She's bummed about the find being moved to Boston and wants the whole town to see the treasures first." Meg rolled her eyes. "She won't quit until every damn person with a beating heart has seen it."

"So you thought you'd drag me down with you?" Lane said.

"Hey, if I'm going down, I'm taking as many people as I can with me. I'm no hero."

Lane laughed. "Charming."

"You always thought so," Meg said, falling straight back into their old pattern but unable to stop. She'd forgotten how easy it was to banter with Lane.

"I thought you were captivating. Especially when you were asleep, snoring like a train," Lane said.

"Hey, I sleep like a lady. You must be confusing me with one of your other conquests."

"Well, you do all sort of roll into one after a while," Lane teased.

Meg punched her lightly in the arm. "Pig."

"Is that why you took a job here? Reminded you of me?"

Meg burst out laughing. "You're an idiot. I forgot that about you."

"I am an idiot. I was an idiot to just let you walk out on me," Lane said.

Meg sighed. "I'm not prepared for this conversation. I've been trying to think how to talk to you all night. What to say to let you down gently. You came all the way here for me, and I acted like a total jackass."

"I see. Meg, you don't need to tie yourself up in knots. Maybe you could let me say what I need to say," Lane said.

"Sure." Meg took a big swig of her drink.

"Right, well…okay, so when we broke up, I sort of pretended I didn't care. Actually, I was heartbroken, and I tried to forget about you, but I couldn't." Lane took a deep breath and carried on, "You made me better. It was like when I was with you, everything made sense, and it was exciting, and I felt like I could do anything. Then you left, and frankly, everything was shit. I'm pretty sure I'm in love with you, Meg."

"Wow. Okay. Pretty sure?"

"Almost certain." Lane nodded.

"Look, Lane—"

"Whatever you say next, don't say, *It's me and not you.*" Lane downed her drink and turned to make another.

"All right, I won't. In truth, it's a little of both. I'm not in any position to have a relationship. We live on different continents, for one thing."

"I can move here. You can move there," Lane said quietly, still not turning around.

"Right. But also I just don't feel that way about you. We're very different people, and it wouldn't work," Meg said softly, as though it would lessen the harshness of her words. And the little voice in her ear that whispered *liar.*

"We worked fine in London."

"We were just fooling around in London. It wasn't meant to be a forever thing. I'm sorry, Lane, if you got the wrong end of the stick."

"You were just passing time with me?" Lane asked.

Was that what she'd been doing? It was certainly what she'd meant to do, before things got complicated. "In a way." Meg winced at Lane's sharp intake of breath. "But also, I liked you. I was—still am—insanely attracted to you. I never meant it to be more than a little fun. I'm so sorry I didn't make that clear to you at the time."

Lane nodded, still with her back to Meg. "I see."

"I never meant to hurt you, Lane. And like I said, a lot of it is about me and not you. I don't have time for a girlfriend. I spend all my time at work. I take any overtime going. I don't have friends, and I haven't been on a date since…wow, since you." Meg hadn't realized that.

Lane turned then with a faint smile on her lips. "You're still saving for your bar in Boston."

"Yes."

"You haven't saved enough yet? I thought you'd been saving since you were nineteen?" Lane asked.

Meg felt defensive. "That's my business. Not all of us are lucky enough to have parents that'll buy us whatever we want."

"I'm sorry. I didn't mean anything by it," Lane said, holding up her hands. "I'd happily buy you any bar you wanted. You could hire all the staff you need—you wouldn't even have to work there."

Meg shook her head. "That's not what I want at all. You just don't get it. You never did."

"Don't get what? Meg, I can offer you everything—buy

you almost anything. You don't have to do this." Lane gestured around the bar.

"But you can't buy me, Lane. I'm not for sale," Meg said and stood up.

"Shit, I didn't mean that. I'm sorry, that wasn't what I meant."

"Yes, it is. Whether you realize it or not, that is exactly what you meant. You're so used to buying whatever you want. It never occurred to you that I wouldn't be for sale too. This is how you were in London. Constantly buying me things, paying for things. And not with money you earned."

Lane blanched, and Meg realized she'd gone too far. She'd meant to be kind, let Lane down gently. At the first mention of money, she'd gone off. It was a sore spot for her, she knew that, but Lane didn't deserve to be on the receiving end of Meg's insecurities.

"Damn it. I'm sorry. I'm tired, and that's no excuse, but maybe we should talk again tomorrow—"

"No. You've said enough. I get the picture, Meg. Thanks for your time." Lane came around from behind the bar and headed for the door. Meg reached for her arm, but Lane shrugged her off. She guessed she deserved that.

"Lane, wait."

But Lane wouldn't. She slid the bolts back and opened the door. "By the way, Meg, I never wanted to buy you, or own you—or whatever you think I wanted. I just wanted to make things easier for you. I know you've struggled your whole life, and I was in a position to make that stop. I believe it's normal behaviour when one person loves another."

Before Meg could answer, Lane was gone.

Damn, damn, damn. That was the exact opposite of how Meg wanted this to go. Why did she have to be so mean? Lane was already in a position of vulnerability, and she'd gone and cut her off at the knees. It was the talk of money. It got to her every time.

Her mother had done her best by her, but they'd been broke. Flat out, thrift shop, food bank, share the bathwater broke. Their clothes had always been clean and if not new, then as close as her mother could get. But Meg lived in fear of classmates finding out just how poor she really was. The excuses she made about why she couldn't go to the mall—three cents in her purse—or to cover for why she hadn't seen a TV show the night before, since they couldn't afford cable.

Meg worked like a dog for her money, and in bitter contrast, there was Lane. Born into a rich family and never wanting for anything her whole life. Never needing to think twice about buying anything. Meg bet she'd flown business class over here to win her back. But it wasn't Lane's fault. She couldn't help what she was born into, any more than Meg could. And Lane was generous. There wasn't a charity bucket in London Lane hadn't put money in. Early on when they'd first met, Meg went to watch her run fifteen miles in mud up to her ass for charity.

No, Lane wasn't a bad person at all. Spoiled? Definitely. Entitled? Maybe a little. But Lane hadn't deserved Meg's sharp tongue. It looked like she'd have another apology to make tomorrow. She'd get a good night's sleep, and then maybe she wouldn't be in such a bad mood.

Meg got up and bolted the door closed.

CHAPTER FIVE

 Outer Cape Echo
1 hour ago

It's official, Provincetown is losing daylight hours. Over the last week Ptown has been in perpetual dusk. Officials from Boston are flying in to investigate the phenomenon Tuesday. The weather is unprecedented in the history of the town, and officials are stumped as to why it has occurred.

---

418 likes   *4 Comments*

Craig Cherry: I'm telling you it's to do with that Viking shit.

Dolores Cab: Shut up, Craig, you moron. It's the government. Everyone knows they mess with the weather.

Craig Cherry: No, you shut up, Dolores. Why don't you go terrify more tourists in your illegal cab.

Dolores Cab: *[We are unable to post your comment because you have been placed in a time out. Your time out will expire in seven days.]*

❖

Lane woke up to the sound of screaming. At first, she thought she'd left the TV on, but when she sat up in bed, the screen was dark. The sound was coming from downstairs. Lane heard a crash and then silence.

What the fuck? Was it some kind of joke? Maybe Ella had seen a mouse? No. No one screamed like that for a mouse.

Lane wasn't sure what to do. She knew she should go downstairs and see what was happening, but those screams… She looked around the room for something to use to defend herself. The best she could come up with was an ugly blue vase. It would have to do. If Ella was hurt, or in trouble, Lane needed to help her.

Lane was sure she was overreacting. She couldn't imagine anything bad happening in this tiny town. It was quaint and picturesque. So why the vase? Just in case, she told herself. Just in case.

Another scream. A crash. Moaning. Lane's insides tightened. She was still wearing her clothes from the day before after getting blind drunk alone in her room, so she put on her shoes and reached for the door handle. She put her ear against the door.

Then she heard it—someone coming up the stairs. Each step creaked, the noise getting louder. Shit. Bugger. What if it was whoever had caused the screaming downstairs? Lane picked up the vase and felt completely unprepared. At least the vase was heavy.

She tried to remember the layout of her floor. There was a bedroom opposite hers and then a short corridor to the left. There was at least one other bedroom down there, she thought, though she wasn't sure.

She heard the door of the other bedroom open. Then a woman's muffled voice. Then the screaming again.

Lane squeezed her eyes shut. Shit, she wasn't a hero. She

wasn't remotely brave. But she couldn't just stand around in here while whoever was out there did God knew what. She felt for her phone in her jeans pocket and pulled it out to call the police. Fuck. It was dead. Why could she never remember to charge the fucking thing?

Lane summoned as much courage as she could, eased open her bedroom door, and tiptoed over to the room across the hall. She hid to one side and poked her head round the door before pulling it back sharply.

She wasn't prepared for what she saw in there. Her brain couldn't properly compute the scene. It was like a slasher film, except with smell. And it smelled bad. It was the smell of rotten meat mixed with the metallic smell of blood. The room was covered in it. On the floor by the bed, about eight feet from where she stood, someone crouched over the body of a woman. Its face was at her stomach, and dear God, it looked like the person was eating her.

But that couldn't be, could it? Lane's brain must be malfunctioning. Or maybe she was still asleep and having a nightmare. Or she was misreading the situation. There had to be another explanation.

Lane stuck her head round again just as the crouching person sat up. They turned their head in her direction. Something that couldn't be entrails—

But what else could they be?

—hanging out of their mouth.

Their face was crimson with blood and they were—

Oh fuck, they were *chewing*.

They were *eating* the other person's *insides*.

This had to be a dream—it had to be.

And now it had seen her.

It let out a low groan and got unsteadily to its feet. It tottered, righted itself, and took a step towards her.

Lane was frozen. She couldn't move. Her brain was screaming at her to run, but her feet wouldn't listen. She was going to die here. This thing that was getting closer was going to do to her what it had done to that other person.

And still, she couldn't move.

It took another step towards her.

Then it stumbled, its feet caught in whatever hung from its mouth—shiny and grey and probably an intestine—and it tripped. Fell flat on its face.

Then Lane's feet moved.

She tightened her grip on the vase and charged. She froze for a second when the thing looked up and groaned again. Lane realized she recognized it—*her*. It made her pause for a split second, but then she brought the vase down on Joanne's head.

There was a crack and a pop as Joanne's head burst open like a melon and splattered up the wall and over Lane. What was left of Joanne's head thumped back down onto the carpet. Did heads do that? Lane thought wildly. Did they just go pop?

Lane looked down at her legs and feet. They were covered in a thick yellowish goo. Where was the brain? The blood?

She gagged and turned away from the bodies. The ugly vase had shattered into a million pieces and lay scattered around Joanne like confetti.

Lane backed up against the wall. Her legs shook, and the world went dark for a second. She forced herself not to faint. Whatever the fuck was going on here wasn't over. The first scream she'd heard came from downstairs. She needed to get down there and get the fuck out of here. Find a police station or a phone, at the very least. But what if Joanne hadn't been alone?

Fortunately, there was another ugly vase in this room. Lane picked it up and headed downstairs.

❖

Meg stepped out onto the street. It was after nine, but the town was dead. Between the cold going around and the weather, she guessed the tourists had headed further along the Cape. She couldn't blame them. Sixty-eight and sunny in Wellfleet while Provincetown struggled along in perpetual gloom.

Didn't help her or the other businesses that relied on the tourist trade, though she couldn't lie and say a quiet shift at the Squealing Pig wouldn't be welcome. Today was supposed to be her day off, but with almost everyone else out sick, she had to go in.

Her boss still hadn't returned Meg's calls, and she was starting to worry. She planned to head to the library to see the exhibition, then call in on her boss and Joanne.

Meg started walking down Commercial. It was too early for most stores to be open, but even so, it was still too quiet, and when you coupled the silence with the dark skies, Meg was kind of creeped out. She walked a little faster.

Somewhere behind her, she heard a scream. Meg almost jumped out of her skin. What *was* that? It didn't sound like someone fooling around—the scream sounded real. Meg looked around her at the darkened stores and even darker alleyways beside them. She stared into the gloom of the alleyway beside the Wired Puppy. She squinted, strained her eyes. It looked like someone was standing back there.

"Hello?" Meg called out.

No answer.

Meg pulled her jacket tighter around her. "Hello, is anyone there?"

Still no answer. Someone was definitely there. She could make out legs and arms and the shape of a head. Someone around her own height. Maybe a woman.

The figure groaned. It shuffled forward. That was enough for Meg, and she bolted.

She pumped her legs and tucked in her arms and sprinted up the street. She was completely overcome by an irrational terror she didn't understand. But her gut was screaming *run*, and her legs obeyed as though Meg really didn't have a say at all in the matter.

By the time she reached the Provincetown Public Library, Meg was blowing hard. She stood by the side entrance, bent forward at the waist and gasping for air.

What the hell was that back there? Who was the weirdo in the alley, and why had she run away like that? Why had Meg been so scared?

"Meg? Meg, are you okay?" Wendy Moon walked through the library doors and put a hand on Meg's back. "Honey, what happened?"

"Something…back there." Meg gulped in air.

"Something was back there? Where?" Wendy looked over her and down the street. "I don't see anything."

Meg shook her head. Her breath was starting to come back, and she stood upright. "I'm sorry, Wendy. I got a little spooked. Someone was standing in the alleyway at the Wired Puppy. I think they were trying to scare me. Asshole."

"Who would do something like that? Are you sure someone was there? It's pretty overcast at the moment. Maybe you imagined it."

"No, they were there. They groaned and did this zombie-type shuffle towards me. I think they were fooling around."

That's what it had been, hadn't it? Some idiot kid trying to scare her. Well, they got her good. Meg didn't think she'd ever run so fast or so far in her life. If she ever found out who'd done it, she'd kick their ass.

"Well, come inside and have a glass of water. You're here for the exhibition, right? I've been really looking forward to showing it to you. Unfortunately something terrible has happened."

Meg followed Wendy inside, but her mind was still on the alley. It was the scream. That's what set her off. Usually she'd have gone right in that alleyway and given the kid hiding there a mouthful.

And she was almost certain now it had been kids fooling around. She guessed Provincetown could be boring if you were a teenager. But that was no excuse to hide in alleys scaring people.

Meg followed Wendy into the main part of the library where tons of books lined shelves. She'd always liked this place. She remembered the first time she'd come here and gone up to the second floor. She'd been stunned and delighted to see a full-sized boat right in the middle of the room. Its masts reached right up to the ceiling. It looked like it was ready to sail right on out of there.

Meg realized Wendy was talking to her. "Sorry, Wendy, what did you say?"

Just as Wendy turned to repeat it, the lights went out.

Someone screamed.

❖

Lane held the vase like she was the last up to bat the last over, and it was for the Ashes. She held the vase by the neck down by her leg, and she edged around the door frame and poked her head in the kitchen just long enough to see no one lurked there.

The room was a mess, though. Chairs overturned and crockery smashed to pieces on the floor. Lane stepped into the doorway proper and nearly slipped on a pastry that had been trampled into the lino.

The kitchen was a slaughterhouse. There was blood up the walls, and a large wet pool of it glistened in the light and covered half the floor. Lying in the centre of the pool was Ella. Her arms were up by her sides, and her mouth hung open. Sightless eyes, partially hooded, stared at Lane. She was definitely dead. Even if it hadn't been obvious from her face, something had been at her stomach. She was torn open from breast to pelvis, and the stink was almost unbearable.

Lane forced herself further into the kitchen. She had to make certain nothing was still in here before she checked the rest of the bed and breakfast. Ella told her yesterday there were four other guests. Excluding the one who now lay dead upstairs, that left two other people. Lane thought they must have heard the screams like she had, but you never knew. They might still be tucked up in bed. Lane just hoped it was somebody else's bed.

Suddenly, Ella twitched. At first Lane thought it was her imagination. Then Ella did it again. A whole body convulsion followed, and Lane ran to her.

"Ella? Ella can you hear me?" Lane knelt by her side. How this was possible, she didn't know, but Ella was definitely still alive. "Ella, stay still. I'm going to call you an ambulance."

Lane went to the wall phone and picked up the receiver. She dialled 9-9-9. Hung up, and dialled 9-1-1. On the other end it rang and kept on ringing. Lane knew this was a small town, but surely they had enough people to staff the emergency service phone lines?

She hung up and dialled again. The same thing happened.

On the floor, Ella groaned. The sound of it chilled Lane,

and she didn't know why. Desperate, Lane dialled 9-1-1 one last time. Ella was going to die if she didn't get an ambulance.

Behind her, Ella groaned again. Lane heard movement and turned from the phone. Fucking hell, Ella was trying to get up. How was that even possible? Her insides—what was left of them—were hanging on the outside, and there was no way she should even be alive, let alone able to stand. But there she was, using the table as support while she got unsteadily to her feet.

"Ella, you need to lie back down—oh fuck, no." Lane almost puked as the remains of Ella's intestines slid out of her stomach and splattered wetly to the floor. Undeterred, Ella started to walk towards Lane, squishing her guts into the floor and soaking her fuzzy slippers in blood and gore.

This wasn't happening.

It just wasn't happening.

Lane thought she must be dreaming. Any minute she'd wake up. She just had to wait it out.

Then Ella lunged at her with a snarl.

❖

Meg could just about see. Although it was dark outside, it wasn't night, and what light there was filtered weakly through the library windows.

"Wendy?" Meg called.

"Yes. Over here," came Wendy's reply.

Meg walked towards the sound of Wendy's voice and found her by a stack of cookery books.

"Did you hear the scream?" Meg asked.

Wendy nodded. "Val Rodman and Celia Avery are the only other people in the library. It must be one of them."

Val and Celia had worked at Provincetown Public Library

for years. From what Meg heard, they'd grown up here and never left. They were best friends apparently.

"Do you know where they are? We should go check on them," Meg said.

"They should be at the front desk or stacking books, but I haven't seen them for a while. Maybe they're out back."

Meg felt a ball of fear lodge itself somewhere low in her belly. The last thing she wanted to do was walk around a dark library, but if Val or Celia was in trouble, they needed to help them. And to find out why the lights had gone out. That was strange in itself. Meg thought about the shadowy figure earlier, lurking in the alleyway. Maybe it hadn't been just a stupid kid. Maybe whoever was lurking in the alleyway had something to do with this.

But that was stupid, wasn't it? This was Provincetown. She'd never felt safer anywhere else she'd lived.

"This way," said Wendy. "We'll go out back and check on Val and Celia."

Meg followed Wendy down the aisles towards the back of the building. They went through a door and into a short corridor with rooms off to the left and right.

"Which one would they be in?" Meg asked. It was even darker back here, and she was spooked.

"I'm not sure. Coffee room to the right," Wendy said and opened the door.

Meg stood behind her, tensed and ready to run. The situation really had her totally creeped out.

"Hello? Val? Celia?" Wendy called out.

But the coffee room was empty. Meg touched the pot, and it was still warm. Two cups sat side by side with a carton of creamer. Val or Celia had been in here recently.

"Let's try the other room," Wendy said.

Meg went back into the corridor, and now she was in the

lead. She didn't like this at all, though she couldn't explain why. Something just didn't *feel* right.

Meg pushed open the door to the storeroom and nearly jumped out of her skin. "Damn, Celia, you gave me a fright," she said.

Celia was standing in the corner of the room. There weren't any windows in here, so only the light from the corridor gave the room any illumination, and it was dim at best. But Meg knew the woman in the corner was Celia. At six feet she kind of stood out. Plus, she was a regular at the Squealing Pig.

"Celia?" Meg tried again. "Are you okay? We heard a scream."

Celia stayed silent.

Wendy pushed past Meg, almost knocking her out of the way. "Hey, Wendy, careful," Meg said.

"Celia?" Wendy ignored her. "Celia, why did the lights go out? Did you trip a switch? Where's Val?"

Celia groaned, and the sound sent shivers up Meg's spine, though she couldn't say why. Something wasn't right. Celia had never been what you'd call a chatterbox, but she wasn't rude either. Maybe she was in shock. Maybe she was hurt. Wendy took a step back, knocking into Meg again and forcing her back into the hallway.

"Watch out, Wendy." Then she focused on Celia. "Celia?" Meg asked. "Celia, what's going on?"

Celia groaned again. Then she turned and lunged at them. There was just enough light for Meg to see her mouth was covered with blood. She turned and ran.

CHAPTER SIX

L ane turned and ran. The Ella…thing couldn't move very fast, thank God, on account of her guts hanging out and tripping her up every few steps. Lane felt like she was in some kind of nightmare, although now she was positive it wasn't one she was going to wake up from.

She bolted out of the B and B and took off up the road like Usain Bolt. She'd already caved one head in this morning and didn't think she had the stomach to cave in another. Plus, who knew what the fuck was going on in this town. She might need to break another head with this vase before the day was over.

And how in the hell could Ella even be breathing, let alone moving? It didn't make any sense. She'd been mauled. And what about Joanne? Yesterday she'd been on death's door, and now she was eviscerating people with her teeth? And how could her head just *pop* like that?

Lane stopped running when she got to Commercial Street. She looked around, half expecting a mob of B and B owners to come shuffling up the road, tripping over their intestines as they went. But the place was empty. Too empty, but what did Lane know about Provincetown? Maybe no one got up before midday. All the same, it was strange. She checked her watch.

Almost ten. Shouldn't shops be open or at least be getting ready to?

Well, she didn't have time to ponder that. She needed to get to a phone, fast. She'd left her mobile phone upstairs in her room. If there was no one out on the streets, then there would be a house or another B and B whose door she could knock on.

Just as Lane turned to walk up the road, all hell broke loose.

❖

Meg heard Wendy behind her—at least, she hoped it was Wendy. Either way, she was getting the hell out of the library. She pushed through the doors and out onto the street and skidded to a stop almost immediately.

What in God's name was that coming up the road? People. It was people, except…except *were* they people? They came from the left, from the direction of the Wired Puppy coffee house. There had to be more than twenty of them. They were moving slowly, shuffling. And moaning. Just like Celia back in the storeroom. What was going on in Provincetown?

As they got closer, Meg could see they'd been mauled. Like, really and truly mauled. Some were missing limbs. Most had chunks of flesh missing. Meg thought she might puke. She turned slightly towards Wendy without taking her eye off them.

"You seeing what I'm seeing?" Meg asked and chanced a glance at her.

Wendy nodded, mouth wide and eyes like marbles. "I…I think so. How are they still even *alive*?"

"I've no idea, but I have a feeling if they're anything like Celia, we don't want them to see us."

Wendy took Meg's arm. "Come on—I know a back way into the library."

"We can't go back in there. Celia," Meg said.

"There's a room we can lock from the inside. She won't be able to get in. I've been storing some of the artifacts from the Viking haul in it. Trust me, it's like Fort Knox."

"What if she's waiting for us back there?" Meg asked.

"What are the other options? We can't go out onto the street. Those...people..."

Wendy was right. What choice did they have? At least locked in the library they'd have some chance of staying safe until help arrived. Out in the street God only knew what might happen.

"Okay, let's go," Meg said and followed Wendy around the back of the library.

❖

Lane ducked into an alley, out of sight. She watched as a stream of what she assumed were once people staggered past in clusters of ten or twelve. They were all messed up like Ella had been. Bits missing from their bodies here and there. One person had half his face gone—looked like someone had shot him. Yellow goo dripped from his head, and then, he fell and didn't get up. He was soon trampled by the others who looked like they didn't even know he was there.

Suddenly, from a house across the street, a woman and a man, both partially dressed in what looked like police uniforms, burst from the front door, both wielding shotguns. Lane watched in fascination as the whole group of people abruptly stopped their shuffling walk up the street, turned as one, then shuffled towards the couple. The woman and the man began shooting.

Lane ducked down, narrowly avoiding a bullet which whizzed over her head.

"Dale, I'm out," she heard the woman shout.

"I've got you covered, Barb," he called back.

Lane poked her head out and watched the man blast into a bunch of the shufflers while the woman reloaded. Lane had to hand it to them—they were great shots. Heads popped and yellow goo flew.

For a moment, Lane thought they were going to get them all, but the number of shufflers was just too great. Lane tightened her grip on the vase and considered coming out of her hiding place to help them. It was obvious they were about to be overrun. But realistically, what could she do, though? Those people had guns, and they weren't going to hold the shufflers off much longer. How much use would Lane's ugly vase be?

Lane could only watch as Dale and Barb were pulled into the mass of people before they disappeared from sight. One of them—Lane thought it was Dale—screamed once. Then there was silence. Most of the shufflers started moving on again, while several stayed to—*oh fuck*—to eat the couple, by the looks of it.

Lane turned her head and vomited into the alley. They were like…zombies. If she didn't know better, she'd think they were bloody zombies. But zombies didn't exist in the real world, did they? It was impossible.

Lane crouched down and waited. She couldn't look any more, but she daren't leave either. The people were shuffling off but not fast enough. And they'd moved quickly when they saw Dale and Barb.

After a moment, Lane poked her head back round. The last of the shufflers had moved on. What was left of the woman and man lay in the street like rubbish. Lane had to do something. Claw back some kind of dignity for them.

As she started to come out of the alleyway, one of them

twitched. It was just like with Ella. And just like Ella, Dale and Barb should be dead. But here they were, twitching and now moving and now trying to stand up.

Zombies, Lane thought. They were fucking zombies.

❖

Meg tried 9-1-1 again. Someone should be answering, but it just kept ringing out. She checked her service and saw she had plenty of mobile signal even in this closet Wendy was trying to pass off as a room. Meg had never been great in small spaces, but this place sucked. It didn't help that Wendy was pacing about like some kind of caged animal.

"Why don't you sit down?" Meg said.

"Pacing helps me think," Wendy said and jolted Meg's shoulder as she walked past. Again.

Meg gritted her teeth and swallowed the urge to yell at Wendy to sit the fuck down. Wendy was as terrified as she was. If pacing kept her calm, who was Meg to give her a hard time? Besides which, with the rest of Provincetown going crazy, she and Wendy might be the last sane ones left.

OMG, Lane. Meg had totally forgotten she was here in Provincetown. Was she okay? The idea of her being hurt made Meg feel sick. She should go find her. She might be—was probably—in trouble. Lane could barely tie her shoelaces.

"Wendy, I need to get out of here."

"It's too dangerous. We should wait until the cops show up," Wendy said.

"They aren't picking up the phone. For all we know they're like the people out there. Which means they aren't coming to help us."

"They can't be. There must be someone. They have guns and training," Wendy said.

"Right, but who expects this? There weren't just a few sick people out there. There were a ton of them."

Wendy shook her head and picked up speed. Back and forth, back and forth. Meg wanted to scream.

"And what would we do out there except end up like them?" Wendy asked.

"I have a…friend here in town. I need to check that she's all right," Meg said and stood.

"The Englishwoman?" Wendy asked.

"How did you—never mind." Meg was still getting used to how small towns worked. Everyone knew everyone else's business. It was better when the tourists were here, but even so, news spread quickly.

"I understand why you want to go to her, honey, I do. But it's too dangerous right now. Let's wait a while. The cops may show up. Or the army. *Someone.*"

Meg didn't doubt that someone would turn up, but how long it would take them might be the difference between life and death for Lane. Meg's experience of Lane in London was that she wasn't exactly self-sufficient. Chances were she'd be running around like a headless chicken right about now.

Lane smashed the vase down on the shuffler's head. "Take that, you piece of shit," she said.

Lane had managed to break into Spiritus Pizza and was fortunate that the shuffler inside hadn't seen her as it ate raw tomato sauce from a container behind the counter. Lane crept up on it and gave it a good old wallop to the back of the head.

The shuffler went down easy enough, but Lane still felt sick about caving someone's head in. She'd never even been in a fight at school, but here she was, murdering random strangers.

The only thing that made it bearable was the fact these people should be dead. The injuries they carried—mostly to their stomachs—were such that no one could reasonably be up and walking around. And they had yellow goo for brains—she could not forget that.

Lane searched behind the counter for a new weapon. This vase had shattered into a million pieces as soon as it came down on the shuffler's head. She found a marble rolling pin, tested the weight, and decided it would do. What she really needed was a gun, like Barb. But she'd never shot one in her life and had no idea where to even get one. And also, the gun hadn't really helped Barb or Dale when it came down to it, had it. But then Lane wouldn't be taking on the zombie hordes by herself. She just wasn't that brave.

As Lane was coming back from behind the counter, she heard a commotion outside. Shit. That didn't sound good.

She crouched on a booth behind the large window at the front of the shop. Outside, a good fifteen people were running down the road. Lane stood up. She couldn't just wait in here and not help. As she opened the door there was a great thundering sound, like the world was being torn in two. Even the people outside stopped running and turned to stare.

Standing in the middle of the street was what Lane could only think of as the chief zombie. He was huge. Lane stopped where she was with her hand on the latch.

The chief zombie had to be at least eight feet tall. There was barely any flesh left on his body, and his bones showed through the thin layer of skin that covered him. Skin that was grey but shone with a weird blue glow. He had plaits coming down either side of his head, but they looked like they could do with a really good conditioner. He should be in that exhibition in the library, Lane thought.

He shouldn't be real, but he was.

Very real and very solid and standing right up the street.

Behind him stood twenty or thirty zombies of the kind Lane had seen before. Recently dead, she guessed, unlike him. He looked like he'd been dead for years.

He spoke—shouted—in a language she didn't understand. The other zombies seemed to comprehend him, though, and they fanned out behind him like an army about to go into battle.

Lane was terrified.

The chief zombie lifted his hands out to the sides, turned his head to the sky, and roared. Lane thought she might wet herself.

OCE **Outer Cape Echo**
3 hours ago

Who's the man in grey? Locals and tourists alike have all been reporting sightings all over Ptown of a tall ghostly man. Is it a hoax or something more sinister? Whatever it is, it has lots of people spooked. Have you seen him? If you have, or you know anything about the malnourished giant, tell us in the comments below.

419 Likes   *3 Comments*

Lou Bellamy: I seen him. He just stands up by the pier when I'm coming in with my boat in the morning. Weird, crazy guy.

Fi Armstrong: It's a hoax. My son's friend's cousin said some kids from his school made the grey man for an art project, and they're moving him all over town to scare people.

Cab Dolores: [*We suspect this of being a duplicate account and your comments have been suspended.*]

Chapter Seven

"What was that sound?" Meg asked. She had a bad feeling. It had been a loud boom, the kind of sound a jet made when it broke the sound barrier. With everything going on today, she knew it couldn't be good.

"I don't know," Wendy said. "But I think you're right. I think we should get out of here."

"And go where?" Meg slid off the stack of boxes she was sitting on.

Wendy picked up her bag. It looked heavy. "The cops. My car is out front."

"What about Lane?" Meg asked. "I can't just leave her. I need to go find her."

"Are you crazy?" Wendy turned abruptly and looked at Meg as though she'd lost her mind. "We don't even know where she is. The best chance she has is if we get to the cops."

"What made you change your mind?" Meg asked. "You were all set on camping out here."

"I needed time to think. And now I have. We can't just stay in here. What if there are more of those…those *people* out there? They'd overrun us."

"But you're okay with going out there where they are?" Meg asked.

"What choice do we have?" Wendy said, tightening the straps on her bag the same way she seemed to be strengthening her resolve.

Meg had to admit, Wendy had a point. They couldn't stay in here forever. In the last hour, the cavalry hadn't ridden into town and saved them. And 9-1-1 wasn't picking up either.

"But, Wendy, if the cops aren't picking up the phone, doesn't that tell you there might be no one there *to* pick up the phone?"

Wendy nodded. "Yes, I thought of that. But they might be holing up like us. And we can't stay here."

Meg sighed. Wendy was right. But Meg couldn't help thinking of Lane out there all alone. Had she heard the boom too? Or was she already dead? The police department was a brisk fifteen minute walk from the library. Presuming she and Wendy made it there and there were some cops who, for whatever reason, weren't picking up the phone, maybe they could get Lane help. Wendy was right in that it was Lane's best hope. What was Meg going to do? Fend off the likes of Celia with a chair leg like she had now?

"Wendy, you said you're storing the Viking shi—stuff in here," Meg said.

"That's right."

"Any chance there's a fucking big sword in the haul?" Meg asked.

Wendy shook her head. "I'm afraid not."

"What about in the exhibition?"

Wendy huffed out a breath. "Weren't you listening? I told you already—someone broke in to the library last night. They stole everything from the exhibition."

"Oh. I'm sorry. But is there nothing in here we can use to fend them off with?"

"No, honey. I told you. It all got stolen. Besides, apart from a knife, it was all trinkets and jewellery."

"Okay, never mind," Meg said. "I guess the chair leg will have to do."

Meg put her ear against the door. She couldn't hear anyone outside. Not that that meant anything. Slowly, she opened the door and held it there with her foot against the bottom, waiting to see if anyone would try and push through. No one did.

Meg opened the door a little farther so she could look down the corridor. It was dimly lit, but she could see nobody lurked in either direction. She pushed the door open a little wider and stepped out.

Meg could feel Wendy pressed against her back, and it felt weird and comforting at the same time.

"Head for the back exit again," Wendy whispered, and Meg nodded. She strained her ears to listen for any strange noises or groans.

Together, they shuffled down the corridor, Meg with the chair leg resting on her shoulder like a bat, and Wendy with her bag held tightly against her chest. Even though Wendy didn't have a weapon, that bag looked heavy enough to brain Celia if she showed up.

Ahead of them lay the fire exit door. So near and yet so far. Meg kept expecting something to jump out at them. A shadowy figure to block their path. She tried to tell herself to stop thinking like that, but she couldn't help it. Her heart beat hard in her chest, and her legs itched to run. Her brain wanted to unleash panic, but she held on as tight as she could.

Finally, they reached the exit door. Meg let out the breath she'd been holding. Wendy did the same, still up against Meg's back.

Meg pushed open the door and stepped out into the dusk.

Out of the corner of her eye, she could a glimpse of movement. Something ran straight at her, and she didn't have time to react.

It hit her hard and knocked the scream right out of her chest. She fell to the ground. The chair leg rolled out of her hand and out of reach. Shit.

❖

Lane saw the door to the library open about the same time the huge grey chief zombie shot a bolt of whatever the fuck was in his mouth at her. She just had time to dodge and pull whoever was coming out of the library to the ground. She prayed it wasn't a shuffler.

She was aware of a second person stepping back inside. That was good. At least they were out of the line of fire.

Lane scrambled up and off the poor person she'd flattened, grabbed their hand, pulled them up, and dragged them back inside the library. She leaned her back against the door, knowing they didn't have much time.

"Lane?"

It was Meg. What were the chances? Pretty good, Lane supposed, seeing as this was where she said she'd be today.

"We have to go," Lane said.

"What do you mean?" Meg asked, not moving.

"She's right," the woman with her said. "He'll break down that door like it's nothing. We need to go out front, to my car. He'll keep coming for us. I'm Wendy Moon, by the way. You must be Lane. Welcome to Provincetown."

Lane looked at the other woman—Wendy. How did Wendy know it was a bloke? And how did she know it would keep coming for them? Lane suspected Wendy knew something about what was going on. But that was for later. Right now, they needed to get away from here.

"Come on, Meg," Lane said and took hold of her hand. Lane tried to pull her along.

"Celia might still be out there."

"We can handle Celia," Wendy said, drawing her bag close again. "Him, not so much."

Meg's grip tightened on Lane's, and she allowed herself to be led to the front of the building.

"Fine, but one of you needs to tell me what's going on."

Neither Wendy nor Lane answered her.

❖

Out front, all was quiet. Lane looked up the street and couldn't see any more zombies. She guessed they were all still around the back of the library with the chief zombie shooting blue shit at stuff.

Meg had stayed silent and passive—not her normal mode at all—and Lane guessed she was in shock. They all probably were. This was beyond anything Lane could ever imagine.

"This way." Wendy hurried to a beaten-up old hatchback parallel parked opposite. Lane wasn't at all sure it would start. The thing looked like it was on its last legs. "She'll start, don't worry. She may be beat-up, but she's as reliable as anything," Wendy said as if she'd read Lane's mind.

The three of them climbed in, Meg in the rear and Lane and Wendy up front. "I need to do something first. Before we go to the police," Lane said.

Wendy started the car. "No, we go straight to the cops. He's going to come out of there any minute—"

"Then I'm getting out," Lane said and opened her door. She knew they didn't have much time before Chief Zombie came out—in fact, why was he taking so long?

Lane felt Meg's hand on her shoulder. "What is it you need to do?" It was the first time she'd spoken, and Lane was relieved she wasn't catatonic or something.

"The little girl—Joanne's little girl. I need to find her," Lane said, remembering how she'd caved her mother's head in. She felt an almost paralyzing sense of guilt. "Joanne is one of *them* now. I need to find her daughter."

"Wendy, head to Joanne's place. We can't leave Lois," Meg said. Her voice was stronger now and more Meg.

"No. We should go to the cops—"

"Wendy," Meg said, "we don't have time for this. I'm not leaving a six-year-old kid to fend for herself. And Joanne needs us too."

"No, Joanne is one of them now. I killed her. With a vase. I had to," Lane said.

Lane felt Meg's hand squeeze her shoulder. "You did what you had to. We can talk about it later. Wendy. Joanne's. *Now.*"

Wendy sighed and put the car in gear. "Fine, but I'm telling you we should be going to the cops."

"We get Lois, and then we get the fuck out of Provincetown. We can drive up to Wellfleet or Hyannis. They're a better bet than the cops here," Meg said.

Lane felt a little lost when Meg's hand left her shoulder, and she sat back in her seat. Lane had barely heard the click of her seat belt when the car suddenly rose up off the ground and was hurled down the street.

Lane grabbed the dashboard and gritted her teeth. The sound of screeching metal drowned out Wendy's screams as they hit the ground and were dragged along the road by some invisible force.

The car had landed upside down, and Lane fumbled with the seat belt clasp. Her fingers, greasy with sweat, kept slipping off the button. Suddenly, the car was lifted up again like a child's toy, and they were hurled into a wall. Lane's teeth clicked as her head snapped back.

"Meg? Meg, are you okay?" Lane tried to twist her head around, but the car had landed up at an awkward angle on its side, with the crushed roof inches from her head.

"Yes. You?" Meg replied.

Lane closed her eyes in relief and swallowed a sob. "I think so. Wendy?"

Beside her, Wendy stayed silent. When Lane looked, her eyes were closed and blood trickled from a small wound to her forehead. Wendy groaned. They had to get out of here. Fast.

"Meg, can you get out?" Lane asked.

"I think so. The window shattered, and I think I can climb through it," Meg said.

"Okay. That's good. Try and—"

Another loud boom. Fuck, the chief zombie was back. Had to be him that sent the car on a magical mystery tour down Commercial, and now he was coming for them.

❖

Meg heard the boom and struggled to free herself from her seat belt. She clambered out through the broken window and immediately saw a problem. Lane's window was directly against the ground, and an unconscious Wendy blocked her path out through the driver's window.

"Get out of here, Meg," Lane called out. "Find Lois and run."

Meg looked up the road. The big grey zombie—he had to be a zombie, right?—was coming, and he had a lot of smaller zombies with him. There was no way she'd get Wendy out in time to let Lane escape. "No. I'm not leaving you."

"Yes you are. I might get lucky. They might think I'm dead and leave me alone. If I can't get out of the car, there's a good chance they can't get *in* the car. Please, run. Find Lois."

Meg ignored Lane and shook Wendy. "Wendy, wake up. Wendy you have to wake up."

Wendy groaned but didn't come to. "Shouldn't have done it," she sleep-muttered.

"Seriously, Meg. *Fuck off.*"

"I'm not leaving you here." Meg couldn't stand the thought of it. Lane had come looking for her. Had pushed her out of the way of that blue bolt or whatever the hell it was back at the library. There was no way she was leaving her here to die. Or worse, to become one of those people.

"You have to. They'll kill you for sure, but me and Wendy might have a chance. Just *go.*"

Meg shook her head, but her resolve was wavering. There was no way she was getting Wendy out by herself. There *was* a chance the zombies would think Lane was dead. And there was a six-year-old out there who might need help.

"Okay," Meg said. "Okay, I'll go. Do you remember the Squealing Pig?" she asked.

"Yes."

"Meet me there. I'll go and get Lois if she's not already left town. You and Wendy head to the Pig."

"Yes. All right. Now *go.*"

Meg took off. She hurried down a side street she knew would take her along the beach. She could get most of the way to Joanne's house without having to come back up onto Commercial. It would involve a little trespassing, but that was the least of her worries right now.

Meg heard another boom as she slipped down the side street. She tried not to think about Lane trapped in the car. Lane would be okay. She had to be.

CHAPTER EIGHT

L ane closed her eyes and took shallow breaths, trying to hide. Would they know anyway? It seemed likely that a being who could shoot blue flames out of its mouth could also tell she was alive.

And then there was Wendy. What if she came to, just as the zombies got to them? If they knew *she* was alive, it would stand to reason they'd check to see if Lane was too.

At least Meg got away. Lane wasn't proud of much in her life, but convincing Meg to leave when she'd been desperate for Meg to stay and help her get out of the car was something. Selfish and self-centred her whole life, she'd finally thought of someone else instead of herself. She'd hold on to that.

The sound of moaning and groaning got louder. Another great boom. Beside her, Wendy stirred. Lane prayed she'd stay quiet.

Past Wendy, through the window, Lane could see feet passing. None of the zombies seemed inclined to stop and investigate the car their leader had kicked up the road like a can. As they streamed past her, she tried to keep a rough count. Looked like about a hundred. A hundred people turned into God knew what by God knew what.

If Wendy came to—and Lane prayed she did—she'd have

some explaining to do. Wendy definitely knew something. The cut on her head had stopped bleeding, and Lane hoped she was only knocked out. If she was properly comatose or whatever, there was no way Lane would be able to take her with her. She reckoned she could drag her as far as the Squealing Pig, but not much further.

Suddenly, the chief zombie was right beside the car. Lane held her breath as it stopped. She could see his bony grey legs. The remnants of what could be boots clung to them in scraps. What the fuck was he?

The seconds ticked by, and he didn't move.

Then, the screeching of metal as something—she guessed *him*—pushed down on the car. Lane closed her eyes and prayed she wouldn't be crushed to death.

A crack as the remaining glass in the windscreen popped and shattered. Still the car was pushed down, and Lane felt her panic build. She wouldn't scream—couldn't scream. She'd wait this out. He didn't know she was here. And being crushed to death was better than the alternative.

Another boom, and then he called out in some foreign and ancient-sounding language. The car rocked as he let go. The zombies began to stream back up the road towards her. He knew she was there. They were going to drag her out and devour her. Just like Barb. Just like Ella.

Lane squeezed her eyes shut. She thought about Meg. Brought her lovely face to mind. Lane imagined her as she had looked that first time they met. When Lane saw her on the stairs. Long dark hair. Beautiful. Meg was beautiful. Lane tried to let that memory be enough as she braced herself to be dragged from the car.

❖

Meg groaned and opened her eyes. Too bright. She squeezed them shut again and pulled the blanket up over her head. Her throat was on fire, and her nose felt like someone had stuffed it full of cement.

There were no two ways about it. She was sick, and it pissed her off. She never got sick—or at least never admitted to it. But there was no way of hiding this. Not even to herself. Her head throbbed, and just the thought of getting up made her want to cry.

She would have to call in sick to work. She hated that because it would mean admitting this thing had her beat. She wasn't due in for a few hours, so she'd sleep a little longer.

Her phone buzzed. She sighed and opened her eyes again. Reached for it off the bedside table. A message from Lane. She shot back a quick reply about being sick and lay back down.

When she woke next, she felt just as terrible but could tell she'd been asleep for hours. Shit. Work would be wondering where she was. She reached for her phone again with her eyes still squeezed shut.

"Hey."

A soft voice and a cool hand on her head.

"Lane? What are you doing here?"

"You said you were sick, in your text," Lane said.

"I didn't mean you had to come over." Meg struggled to sit, and Lane gently held her down.

"I wanted to. I brought medicine and stuff. Soup. And Mountain Dew. I remember you said you liked that when you were sick."

Despite feeling like someone had run her down and backed up over her, Meg felt something warm inside her. She wasn't used to being taken care of. Usually would have railed against it. But with Lane, being cared for was welcome. She liked it. It made her feel safe.

Meg started to drift off to sleep again.
"I'll be here when you wake up. I bought chicken soup."
Meg felt a smile ghost onto her lips as she fell asleep.

❖

Meg tried to ignore the sounds coming from down the street. She tried not to think about Lane and Wendy trapped in the car or what might be happening to them. She also tried not to think about how badly she'd misjudged Lane. She'd forgotten about the time Lane took care of her when she'd been sick. Maybe she'd blocked out a lot of the good things Lane had done. She didn't want to think about why that might be, either.

Meg pushed on Joanne's front door, and it swung open. Not locked. Not good. She didn't want to risk calling out in case there was one of those people inside. She prayed Lois was with her aunt and well out of Provincetown. There was a chance Joanne had done as she'd promised and called her sister.

Meg walked down the hall trying not to make a sound. She couldn't help the floorboards that squeaked and hoped if there was someone in here, they wouldn't notice. From her experience in the library, the zombies—or whatever they were—didn't seem to notice you until you were on top of them. She doubted one would be standing there waiting to ambush her, but you never knew.

Meg stuck her head round the living room door. A sofa was overturned, and a vase of flowers lay crushed into the carpet. There'd been a struggle—or maybe a chase. She followed the trail of flower gunk into the bathroom at the back. It ended abruptly by the bath. No one lurked behind the door.

In Lois's bedroom, things lay undisturbed, and Meg

was relieved. Either the little girl was gone, or the struggle hadn't happened in here. Joanne's bedroom was another story altogether. The stink was like a wall. Meg imagined it seeping into her clothes and her pores, and she started to gag.

The bed was soiled—soaked in gore, more like. Sheets pushed back and pillows tossed to the floor. A sticky stain spread out from the bed to the door. Meg didn't want to think about what that might be. She thought maybe Joanne had died and come back to life in here. Jesus, she hoped Lois had been gone by the time Joanne died.

The sound of scraping came from the hallway, and Meg's heart rate kicked up. What the hell was that? She turned around in time to see legs dangling from the loft. Then someone dropped down. She'd forgotten about the loft. Easy place to hide. Too late, she'd realized her mistake.

❖

Lane felt the vibration before she heard it. It came as a quiet rumble and then built in volume until it was a roar. At first, she thought it was him, the chief zombie. Then she realized the sound was coming from further up the road, and that the other zombies were ignoring their car completely and shuffling towards the noise.

Beside her, Wendy groaned again and opened her eyes. Lane tried to turn her head towards where the noise was coming from, but the seat headrest was in the way. Outside the car, the chief zombie moved away from them. Lane took a chance.

"Wendy," she whispered. "Keep still. He's right outside the car."

Wendy groaned once more and nodded.

Lane watched as the chief zombie followed his minions

down the road. She guessed they could see where the noise was coming from. It sounded like an engine. A big one. Lane hoped it was a bloody great tank.

"Wendy, do you think you can climb out of the car? Out the window by you?" Lane whispered.

Wendy nodded. "I think so. My head hurts."

"I know it does. But we need to go before they come back."

"Okay." Wendy unclipped her seat belt and pushed herself up. She held on to the frame of the car and dragged herself out.

Lane followed quickly. In the distance, she could see the zombies shuffling towards something. It was shiny and getting closer. What the fuck was it?

"Come on, we need to get out of here. Meg's going to meet us at the Squealing Pig." Lane watched as Wendy reached back into the car and pulled at her bag. It was caught on something inside the car. Lane kept looking back up the road. "Wendy, hurry."

"One second."

"Wendy, *now.*"

Up ahead, Lane could see the vehicle attracting the zombies was a bus in blue and chrome. It knocked zombies out of the way like skittles.

"One second," Wendy repeated, just as she pulled her bag clear. She stumbled slightly.

"Shit, look at that." Lane watched as the bus got closer. It had to be doing forty, and it was splattering zombies like bugs. For a moment, Lane thought it was going to make it through the horde. The bus weaved back and forth across the road. *It's trying to hit them*, Lane realized and gave a silent cheer. It was almost through the horde, almost clear.

Then, much like their car had been manipulated, the bus rose up from Commercial Street, flipped over, and shot along the road on its side like a toy. It spun around, taking out cars and porches and shop windows in a deafening, screeching, crashing roar.

"Wendy, run!" Lane shouted as the bus careened towards them.

Lane took off at a sprint. She ran into one of the narrow side streets and headed to the beach. When she looked back and saw Wendy struggling to keep up, she slowed down. Behind them, Lane heard the terrible sound of metal twisting and grinding. There was a loud bang, then the acrid smell of smoke. It didn't take a genius to work out what had happened.

Lane pulled up short, and Wendy crashed into her back. Wendy's bag hit Lane in the side. "What the bloody hell have you got in there?" Lane asked and rubbed her bruised ribs, which stung. Wendy didn't answer. From the weight, Lane would have said bricks, but things inside the bag clinked and clanked like cutlery.

The tide was in, leaving barely three feet of beach. "We'll have to wade through it. Cut around back, to the Pig," Wendy said.

The freezing water took Lane's breath away. But this was better than being eaten alive. The water came up to her knees, and pretty soon her teeth were chattering.

"How are you doing, Wendy?" Lane asked.

"Fine. My head's stopped bleeding," Wendy answered.

Lane looked back at Wendy, who was doing her best to stay upright with her bag held above her head.

"Wendy, why don't you lose the bag? It'll make life easier," Lane said.

"No, I can't. It has my purse and keys in it," Wendy replied.

Lane opened her mouth to point out Wendy probably wouldn't be needing either for a while. She changed her mind.

Maybe hanging on to the bag was helping Wendy hold on to something normal. God knew Lane was struggling to process the situation herself.

And how was Meg coping? Had she made it to Joanne's? No, she couldn't think about it. Meg would be fine. She was probably already in the Squealing Pig waiting for them. The thought of anything else made Lane want to throw up.

"Hey, you guys zombies?"

Lane looked up at the sound of the voice. They'd made it to the alley by the hardware store, Lands End Marine Supply, and a woman was now standing at the top of the alley.

The woman wielded a rifle slung over one shoulder and a baseball bat in each hand.

"No. We aren't," Lane said.

"That's what I figured. You aren't missing any body parts. Wendy, that you?" The woman looked past Lane to Wendy, who was squeezing water out of the top of her tights.

"Hi, Teensy. It's good to see you," Wendy said, barely glancing up.

Teensy? One thing this woman mountain was not was teensy, Lane thought.

"Who's this?" Teensy asked, pointing a bat at Lane.

"That's Lane. My bag is wet. How did my bag get so wet?" Wendy asked.

"Just you two?" Teensy asked.

"And Meg. She's meeting us at the Squealing Pig," Lane said.

Teensy frowned. "You left her by herself?"

"Not exactly. It's a long story." Lane started walking up the alley again. "We should get inside. I'll tell you there."

"I guess I could use a beer." Teensy slung a bat over each shoulder and led them up the alley.

Lane shrugged and followed her. A beer sounded good to her as well.

"You coming, Wendy?" Lane asked.

"I need a new bag."

Wendy's obsession was starting to worry Lane. Maybe she'd really hit her head hard and lost her mind.

"We can deal with that later," Lane said.

"No, now. I'll drop into Marine Supply real quick," Wendy said.

"Wendy, for fuck's sake." Lane threw up her hands.

"Hey, don't speak to Wendy like that," Teensy said. "She wants a new bag—we can make a quick trip. Besides, you two are soaked. You should change into some dry clothes."

Lane couldn't deny Teensy's logic. "Fine, but I don't think we should be long. Those zombies seem to like staying up on the main road."

"I just need a new bag is all. And some dry clothes," Wendy said.

"Wendy wants a bag, so a bag she shall have. Those zombies show up, I'll pop their heads like grapefruits. The big one shows up, though, and we run," Teensy said.

"Fine. Let's get Wendy a new bag. Then after, once we get to the Squealing Pig, Wendy can tell us what's going on here."

Lane saw Wendy's head come up sharply. "I don't know any more than you do."

"I don't think that's true," Lane said. "You seemed to know quite a bit at the library."

Wendy shook her head. "That was common sense. That other…*man* was huge. Anybody with any sense would have known to run away."

Again, Lane couldn't deny the logic, but something

was bothering her. She couldn't explain it, but she just had a feeling Wendy knew more than she was saying. The fact she was denying it left Lane with even more questions. Once they were in the Squealing Pig, she and Meg would discuss what to do. If Meg made it. If they made it.

"You coming?" Teensy asked Lane.

"Yeah, sorry. I'm coming," Lane said and followed the other two up to Lands End Marine Supply.

❖

Meg regarded the little girl in front of her. She looked scared but not traumatized. She was dirty but didn't have any injuries that Meg could see.

"You could have hurt yourself jumping from up there, Lois," Meg said.

Lois shrugged. "Could have hurt myself being eaten by zombies too."

The kid had a point. "What happened?" Meg asked.

"My mommy got real sick. She didn't call a doctor like she promised. I got scared from all the groaning, so I hid in the attic," Lois said.

"How did you get up there?"

"On there." Lois pointed to a dresser against the wall. "I climbed up and then pushed the hatch open. It's real easy. Want me to show you?"

"No, that's okay. Lois, you need to come with me. I'm going to get you out of here," Meg said and reached for the little girl's hand.

"But there's zombies out there. I've seen them. Can't we stay here? In the attic?" Lois clutched Meg's hand but wouldn't move.

"I know, honey. But I promise I won't let them get you. We can't stay here. I have friends waiting for us," Meg said and hoped she wouldn't be proved a liar.

"What friends?" Lois asked, still not moving. She was pretty strong for a small kid.

"Well, you met one of them today. Her name is Lane. And there's Wendy."

"You're all that's left? There's nobody else?" Lois asked.

"I'm sure there are others. Maybe they're lying low, or maybe they got out of Provincetown already." Meg prayed Lois wouldn't bring up her mom. What would she say to her?

"It's okay, I know about my mom," Lois said as if reading her mind. She glanced down at her feet. "She's one of them now, isn't she?"

Meg pulled Lois into a hug. "I'm sorry, honey. I'm so sorry."

She felt Lois's small arms reach around her back. They had a little time, Meg guessed. She could give Lois a little time to grieve her mother.

Meg was all Lois had now. The thought hit her like a ton of bricks. The kid was totally reliant on Meg to get her out of this alive.

The truth was she couldn't protect Lois, not really, not any more than she could protect herself. Her mind went to Lane, trapped in that car with Wendy. Was Lane a zombie now? Shuffling around Provincetown? Meg prayed not. Just thinking about it made things tear loose inside her. And now she had Lois to take care of. She couldn't think about it. She had to believe Lane was waiting with Wendy in the Pig for her.

Meg crouched down in front of Lois. "Honey, we have to go now. Do you trust me?"

Lois looked right in her eyes and nodded. "Yes. I trust you."

Meg could see she did. The way most little kids trusted adults to take care of them, completely and totally. And just like that, Meg knew that whatever happened, she would get Lois out of here. Or die trying.

CHAPTER NINE

Lane would never admit it, but the visit to Lands End Marine Supply was a good idea. Her jeans, shoes, and socks were soaked through. Plus, the jacket she had on was not at all warm. Lane put the new items in her bag. She didn't feel comfortable changing in the middle of the shop. They were too exposed, and she wanted to be somewhere safe.

Being in Lands End Marine Supply with Wendy and Teensy while the world went to shit outside was an exercise in weird. The two of them were acting like they were on a little shopping trip. Teensy bowled straight in and shouted at the top of her lungs, "Any of you fucking nasty zombies are in here, I'm going to pop the yellow goo right out of your heads."

"Teensy," Lane hissed, "what are you doing?"

"Making sure those creepy shitheads know we're here," Teensy said and started eying up shovels near the entrance.

"And what if there's loads of them? You're going to fight them all off by yourself?"

"Sure. I was a marine for fifteen years. These assholes don't bother me a bit." Teensy smiled at Lane, and there was nothing friendly about it. "They've fucked up my town. I'd love a crack at a few more of them."

"And what if they're here with the chief zombie?" Lane asked.

Teensy frowned. "He's a different story. We'd probably be best off running if he's here. But if he was, he would've zapped us already." Teensy held out one of her baseball bats and pointed it at Lane. "Pow."

Lane grinned. "Pow?"

"Yeah. Pow. I'm not an idiot. My baseball bats aren't going to do a damn thing against him. You ever seen anything like that before?" Teensy asked.

"Never in my life. But then, I've never seen a regular zombie before either," Lane said.

"You make a good point. How do you think they got here? Experiment gone wrong?"

Lane had no idea, but she knew someone who probably did. She turned to the aisle where she'd last seen Wendy.

"Where did Wendy go?" Lane asked, realizing that Wendy had disappeared.

"Probably to get a new bag. That's why we're here. You should get some new pants and shoes. Don't want to get sick." Teensy grinned.

Lane couldn't help but laugh. "God forbid I catch a cold. Meet you back here in five minutes?"

"Sure. Scream if you need us," Teensy said.

Lane walked down the tightly packed aisles. There was a lot of stuff here. Tools, cleaning products, and dog food sat side by side with waders, hats, jeans, and boots. There were sweatshirts and fishing rods, key rings and camping chairs.

Lane found a pair of sturdy looking boots in her size and put them on. They weren't exactly her style, but they were waterproof and dry. She found some jeans that didn't look terrible and a soft, warm sweatshirt. She decided to pick up a bag herself, a claw hammer, and a mallet. She'd need to get close to use them as weapons, but currently she only had bare hands, so anything was an improvement on that.

Lane had figured out that popping their heads killed them—or whatever a zombie version of death was—so knives would be no good. And she wanted something she could wield easily enough. She wasn't small but she wasn't built like Teensy. She paused a moment, realizing she was deep in thought about picking out the best implement to kill someone with. What the fuck had happened to her life? She'd come to Provincetown to get Meg back, and now here she was, testing the weight of a mallet, trying to decide if it was heavy enough to smash through bone and brain matter.

And what about Meg? Was she safe? Did she reach Joanne's apartment? Lane couldn't contemplate the idea she hadn't. But then, when it came to Meg there was a lot Lane wouldn't contemplate. Had she been a fool to come here and try to win Meg back? Meg's reaction said she was, but all the same, Lane couldn't find it in herself to regret the decision. Especially in light of recent events. Lane didn't consider herself a hero, but she knew she'd lay down her life for Meg in an instant.

And if she would do that, then maybe she wasn't the coward she'd always thought she was. Maybe there was a lot more to her than she thought. She'd already fought for her own life several times to get here.

All she needed now was for Meg to be okay. Meg was a survivor. Even back in London Lane knew that. There was a toughness to Meg that she'd always admired. There was also a wall around Meg that Lane found pretty much impossible to break down. She wondered if maybe the two went hand in hand. If maybe Meg wasn't able to have one without the other.

Once she was happy with the items she'd chosen, Lane

went back to the front of the shop and waited for the others. She could hear them near the back. What was taking them so long? All Lane wanted to do was get to the Squealing Pig and see if Meg was there yet.

Part of her wanted to head straight over to Joanne's house. But they'd agreed to meet in the Pig, and Lane had to believe Meg would be there.

They needed to make a plan. Surely it wouldn't be long before people outside Provincetown realized something was wrong. They'd send in the army or something. All Lane and Meg had to do was wait it out. Lie low until the cavalry arrived. Leaving was too risky. They'd seen what the chief zombie could do to cars. And to the bus. Lane wondered who'd been on the bus. And whether any of them had survived. She hoped so but doubted it.

Behind her, a bell tinkled as the shop door opened. Lane turned, hoping it was Meg. It wasn't. All she could think before she raised her hammer was that Teensy was going to be happy.

❖

Meg led Lois along the beach. For some reason, the zombies didn't seem to come down to the waterfront. They preferred the main streets. She guessed maybe because that's where most people were. In all the movies she'd seen and books she'd read, she never heard about a zombie who was afraid of water.

Just as they were coming up the side of the Lands End hardware store, Lois stopped.

"What's up, honey?" Meg asked.

"Can't you hear that?" Lois looked towards the store with her eyes wide.

"Hear what?" Meg couldn't hear a thing.

"There's zombies in there." Lois shivered and Meg pulled her close.

"We'll be real quiet so they don't hear us. Okay?" Meg ran her hand over Lois's head. She felt her nod.

"How can you even hear them?" Meg whispered.

Lois shrugged. "My mommy says I have bat ears."

Meg didn't comment on Lois's use of present tense. The kid had enough going on trying to process her town suddenly filling with zombies. Besides, she knew Joanne was gone. Meg didn't need to remind her.

"Come on," Meg whispered again.

They made it to the Squealing Pig. Meg still had her key, but she didn't need it. When she pushed on the door, it swung open. She felt her heartbeat speed up.

Meg moved Lois behind her and stepped inside. She hefted the rock they always used to hold the door open. Just in case.

"Lois, can you hear anybody through there?" Meg pointed to the bar.

"No. At least, nobody shouting," Lois said.

Meg inched forward, painfully aware she had nothing to defend either Lois or herself with.

She rounded the corner into the bar. Men's and ladies' rooms were to the left, and she spared them a quick glance. She doubted zombies would have the wherewithal to hide, but she'd found Celia in the storeroom back at the library. She guessed one could be back there. But first things first. She had to make sure the bar was clear.

"Lois, you wait here. If you see or hear anything, I want you to run to the beach."

"Okay."

Lois gripped the back of Meg's jacket, and they shuffled forward. In the bar, something crashed to the ground. Then, the sound of a low groan.

❖

Lane swung again and connected with the woman's head. She tried hard to push the idea that this was a woman out of her head. Someone who'd once loved and laughed. Lane swung again, and the zombie went down.

Behind her, Teensy let out a war cry. Lane turned and watched her belt a zombie so hard her bat snapped. The woman was fucking mental, but thank God for her.

Wendy was probably cowering in a corner somewhere. But Lane didn't blame her. She'd do the same if she could.

"Lane," Teensy called, "heads-up."

Lane turned around just in time to see a zombie lunging for her. She took a step backwards and tripped. She pinwheeled her arms in an effort to stay upright, and the hammer flew out of her hand.

It was no good. She fell. The zombie followed her down.

❖

Meg shoved Lois back out into the short corridor. "Run."

She didn't look back to see if Lois had obeyed her. Instead, she went left into the kitchen. There would be something in there she could use to defend herself.

She pulled up short when she saw two zombies in there. They had their backs turned, and she was sure they didn't know she was here.

Yet.

Meg went back out the way she'd come and saw Lois waiting by the door. "I told you to run."

"I did. They're out there too."

"What?" Meg pushed past Lois and opened the door a crack.

Lois was right. She managed to push the door shut just as one zombie lunged at her. She slammed the deadbolt into place.

What were they going to do? They were effectively trapped. She had no idea how many zombies were in the bar. But even if there was just one, that still made it three against one.

Meg squeezed her eyes shut and tried to think. The doors out front would be locked. Not enough time to open them and get out. Unless…

She turned and crouched in front of Lois. "Honey, I need you to listen very carefully and do exactly as I say."

Lois nodded and bit her lip.

"We're going to make a run for it. You'll need to stay real close to me. When I say so, I want you to run for the front door, unlock it, and take off. Just keep running, okay?"

Lois shook her head. "What about you?"

"Don't you worry about me. I want you to run and hide and wait for the army or the cops or whoever the fuck comes." Meg gripped Lois's shoulders. "Promise me."

"I don't want to leave you," Lois whispered.

"You have to. We're in a bit of a bind here. I know your mom would want you to be okay. Wouldn't she?"

Meg knew it was a bit of a low blow, but Meg needed Lois to do what she said. It was unlikely both of them were getting out of here alive, and Meg didn't see any other way.

"Lois?"

"Okay. I promise."

Meg pulled Lois into a hug and gathered the courage to do what she had to next.

❖

Lane was sure it was curtains for her as the zombie bore down. She kicked out in an effort to dislodge it, but the zombie took the blow and probably a couple of cracked ribs with equanimity. She tried to turn and crawl, but it landed on her and took all the wind out of her.

Lane clawed at the scuffed lino in an effort to drag herself away. It was no good. She felt the zombie's rancid breath tickle her cheek and ruffle her hair. The smell was awful. Wet and warm and rotten.

Suddenly, it was gone. Tossed aside like it weighed nothing. Lane jumped up and saw Teensy grab it by the scruff of the neck and seat of its pants and launch it across the shop and into a display of tents.

"You okay there, Lane?" Teensy called out.

"Yeah. Fine. Thanks."

"No bites?"

Lane looked down at herself. A smear of something across her belly. She lifted her shirt. Dry underneath. No wounds. She sighed with relief and swallowed.

"No. I'm good."

"Get your hammer then. I just saw a bunch of those suckers head over to the Pig. Isn't that where we're meeting Meg and the little one?"

"Yeah." Lane pulled off her sweatshirt, grabbed a hoodie from a nearby rack, and picked up her hammer. "Let's go."

❖

Meg stood. She turned to face the bar. She felt behind her for Lois and made sure she was fully shielded. Maybe whoever was out there wouldn't see her at all. The zombies seemed to act like brainless machines. It wasn't clear how much awareness they had, but Meg was fairly certain it wasn't a lot.

Meg took one step forward. Something hit the door behind her hard. Lois screamed.

In the kitchen, a zombie groaned.

Something hit the door again. The door split by the lock.

"Meg."

Was she hearing things?

"Meg, if you're in there, open the door."

Meg looked down at Lois. "You hear that too?"

Lois nodded.

Relief flooded Meg. She slammed the deadbolt back, turned the knob. Something grabbed her hair from behind and pulled.

Meg fell just as the door opened. She twisted and rolled as something fell on her. The stink made her eyes water. A hand, soft and sticky, trailed across her cheek.

Then, it was gone.

Above her, Lane swung a hammer and clocked a zombie clean in the head. Yellow goo exploded out of its head and hit the wall. Meg rolled out of the way, then stood.

Behind Lane, Teensy—what was she doing here?—was trying to shut the door, but at least two zombies were pushing their way in. Meg went to help.

"Grab that rifle off my shoulder," Teensy grunted.

Meg pulled it loose.

"Now I'm going to let go of the door, and you're going to start shooting. You know how to shoot?" Teensy asked.

"I do." Meg didn't see the point in telling her she'd shot competitively for her state once upon a time.

"Okay, on three."

Meg raised the gun.

"One," Teensy said.

Meg nestled the butt in her shoulder.

"Two."

Meg closed one eye and angled her head.

"Three."

Teensy opened the door and Meg started shooting.

OCE **Outer Cape Echo**
1 hour ago

Is there no end to Provincetown's strange weather? This morning the ferry was cancelled and boats were turned back from Boston. Officials say the water is so dangerous they've issued a ban on any vessels crossing over until further notice. Weather experts are baffled as to why Provincetown is experiencing such extreme conditions. Is it a freak event or something more sinister? Reports are coming in that power and internet are also down in the tiny seaside town.

421 Likes   *4 Comments*

Rachel Smith: I haven't been able to contact my sister since yesterday. Any word on when the power will be back up?

Tom Moore: My cousin called me last night saying something weird was happening over there. When are the authorities going to go and take a look?

Janet Jones: I drive the bus from Hyannis, and we got

cancelled today. I'm thinking about driving over there and seeing what the hell is going on. I'll be making my usual stops if anyone wants to join me.

Cara Barrett: Must be something up. *Dolores Cab* hasn't been on here trolling anyone yet.

❖

As soon as Meg stopped firing, Lane and Teensy waded in and started hitting the two zombies Meg hadn't managed to shoot in the head. Meg was a great shot, Lane realized. She'd put down three without even blinking. All shots to the head. Lane realized the old zombie movies had been correct. You had to hit them in the head.

When the zombies were dead, and they made sure they'd cleared the Pig, Lane allowed herself to feel the relief that washed over her. Meg was safe. Lois was safe. Maybe everything would be okay.

"You okay, Meg? Not bitten?" Teensy asked from behind Lane.

Meg squeezed Lane's arm as she walked past and hugged Teensy. "I'm fine. No bites. What about you guys?"

"We're good," Teensy said. "You're some shot with that rifle. You got three of them right between the eyes."

"Junior State Champion," Meg said and laughed.

Teensy squeezed her again with one arm, and Lane felt a spark of jealousy at the easy affection between them. She had no right, but she felt it all the same.

"Of course you were. Any idea what happened in Ptown?" Teensy asked. "I woke up this morning, went out for my coffee, and then *bam*, some asshole tried to bite my face off."

"Val tried to bite mine," Meg said.

Lane didn't want to talk about her first encounter because Joanne's child was standing right there. Not that anyone was paying Lane much attention.

"I was with Meg when it happened," Wendy said. "It's just awful. I can't believe it's happening."

"Agreed," Teensy said. She gave Meg one more squeeze, and then went over to the windows at the front of the Squealing Pig. "We need to get this place boarded up and secured. No telling when they might come back."

"Then maybe we can work out what the bloody hell to do," Lane said.

They boarded up the windows by stacking tables in front of them. Teensy found some wood from somewhere and nailed it across the doors.

They kept one light on low. They didn't feel safe exactly, but they felt safer. And there were five of them. Not that Wendy was much use, but still. Five were better than one.

Lane popped the tops on four beers and put them up on the bar. She got a ginger ale for Lois and popped that top too.

"Hiding here was a good idea. How long do you think it'll be before the authorities realize something's wrong?" Lane asked.

"Well, it's only just after two p.m. now. Probably take those idiots a while to get their asses into gear," Teensy said and took a long drink.

"So the plan is we just wait here for them?" Wendy asked.

"I guess. We don't have much choice. We've been lucky so far. But there's a ton of zombies roaming around out there," Meg said.

"I saw a load of people get taken out by them this morning. I don't fancy our chances if we keep running around," Lane agreed.

"I don't know." Teensy drained her beer. "Seems kind

of passive to sit around waiting to be saved. I've got a boat. Down at the harbour."

Lane glanced at Lois, who was quietly sipping her ginger ale. "If it was just us, maybe I'd agree."

"That grey dude is bound to make a reappearance soon. I don't know if our little barricade can keep him out." Teensy went behind the bar and grabbed another beer.

"I vote we sit tight. Give it a few hours," Meg said.

"Sure. I can do that." Teensy popped the top and leaned on the bar. "But if that blue-flame-zapping fucker shows up, we run. Down to the harbour. Boat is called *Dawn's Crack*. It's right at the end of the pier."

Lane coughed and spat out her beer. Meg thumped her on the back, and when Lane looked at her, she could see Meg was trying not to laugh.

"Agreed," Lane said, when she finally got her breath back. "If he comes back, we'll escape in *Dawn's Crack*."

Meg did start laughing then.

Teensy looked at them with raised eyebrows. "Something funny about my boat?"

"No, not at all," Lane said, still laughing.

"Oh, come on, Teensy. *Dawn's Crack*?" Meg said.

Teensy grinned and winked at Meg. "Named her after my first love."

"Not Dawn Truman?" Wendy piped up from the table where she sat.

"She was Dawn Ball back then." Teensy sipped her beer. "We were together three months. Then I shipped out, and she married Dan Truman. Broke my heart."

Wendy snorted. "Sure it did. I've never known you to stay with one woman more than a month."

"I was with you a whole year," Teensy said and drained the rest of her beer.

Lane's mouth dropped open. "You and…*Teensy*?"

"Close your mouth, girl—you'll catch flies," Teensy said.

"Sorry, I just…" Lane trailed off, aware she was digging herself a big hole.

Meg nudged her shoulder. "Go on. You just what?"

Lane elbowed Meg back gently. "Nothing at all."

"You didn't think I was gay?" Wendy asked.

Truthfully, Lane hadn't thought about Wendy's sexuality at all. But seeing her and Teensy together, she just couldn't picture it. "It's not that, Wendy," she said.

"Go easy on her, Wendy. Lane's dug herself a big old hole, and she's trying to get out of it." Teensy laughed. "Me and Wendy had some great times. Real chemistry."

Lane didn't want to think about Teensy and Wendy's chemistry. "Lovely."

"Teensy, stop. Little ears." Wendy nodded towards Lois, who was watching the back and forth from her bar stool.

"Whoops. Sorry, kiddo," Teensy said. "You want another ginger ale?"

"I think one's enough. We should eat soon," Meg said.

It made Lane painfully aware she hadn't eaten since yesterday, and she was starving. Her stomach rumbled on cue.

"Make it something cold," Wendy said. "We don't want to attract them here."

Lane nodded. "You have stuff for sandwiches?" she asked Meg.

"Sure."

"I'll help," Lane said.

Behind her, as they walked into the kitchen, she heard Teensy say, "I bet you will."

Lane glanced back in time to catch Teensy wink and grin.

Chapter Ten

Lane couldn't see out the window. They'd piled tables in front of them. And in front of the door. As long as the zombies tried to come through from Commercial, they would be fine. Their defences would hold.

The back was trickier. Like Teensy said, they couldn't block up all their escape routes. But the zombies had come through the side alley, so it made sense they would again.

Even though Lane had initially been in favour of waiting it out for the authorities to arrive, she was beginning to feel like a sitting duck. Her gut was telling her they should leave, but she wasn't used to trusting herself. Mostly, she'd relied on other people's advice, but that hadn't been life or death situations. So far in this waking nightmare, she'd done okay. Maybe she could back herself to make decisions and trust her instincts. And all her instincts were telling her they should get out of here.

Lane turned her attention to Meg, who was alone at the bar, the plates from their sandwiches piled beside her. Her head rested in one hand, and she kept nodding off then jerking awake again.

"Why don't you lie down for an hour?" Lane said.

Meg raised her head and blinked slowly. "I don't think that's a good idea. It doesn't feel safe to fall asleep."

"I'll watch over you." The words were out of Lane's mouth before she could stop them. She winced. How pathetic did that sound?

To her relief, Meg smiled. "I know you would, but all the same, I'd rather stay awake."

Lane nodded. Once Meg made up her mind, there was no changing it. She turned her attention to Wendy instead.

Wendy sat at one of the few tables they hadn't used in their barricade. Her new bag—annoyingly, the same bag Lane had chosen—was clutched tightly to her chest. Lane didn't want to dwell on the fact she and Wendy had similar taste. Although, in her defence, Lands End Marine Supply wasn't exactly high fashion, so maybe she could give herself a break.

Lane was interested in what Wendy had *in* her bag, though. And she still needed to follow up on her sneaking suspicion that Wendy knew more about what was happening than she was letting on. She simply could not get past the way Wendy'd reacted to the grey man at the library.

Lane got up and went to sit with Wendy. She slid onto the bench next to her. "Hey, Wendy."

"Hi." Wendy stared straight ahead.

"How are you doing?" Lane asked. She reached out to touch Wendy's hand where it rested on the bag. Wendy squeezed Lane's hand briefly, then went back to clutching the bag. "Wendy?"

"About the same as you, I imagine. This whole situation is"—Wendy threw up her hands—"indescribable. I think, maybe I did something…oh, I don't know. It doesn't matter."

Lane studied Wendy. She was certainly struggling with something, and Lane had an idea she knew what. She'd been guarding that bag with her life, and Lane had an idea maybe Wendy had the Viking treasure in it.

"We'll get out of here, right? We'll be okay?" Wendy asked.

"I don't know," Lane said. "Wendy?"

"Yes?"

"Tell me what's going on in Provincetown."

Wendy flinched. "I don't know what you're talking about."

"The man shooting blue flames out of his mouth. Who is he?" Lane asked.

"How the hell would Wendy know?" Teensy bellowed from her position on the floor. She was playing marbles or something similar with Lois.

"I think Wendy might know a lot more than she's letting on," Lane said.

"Don't be ridiculous," Wendy said. "Why would I know any more than you?"

"Back at the library. You weren't at all surprised to see him, if I remember," Lane said.

"Don't be stupid. How would I know what—who—he is?"

"You've curated the Viking exhibition, haven't you? You're a historian."

"Yes, *Vikings*. Not *zombies*," Wendy said.

"I'm warning you, Lane. Leave her alone. She says she doesn't know anything, she doesn't know anything. Besides, why would she? Bunch of fucking zombies running around. Why would Wendy have a clue about that?" Teensy shook her head and picked up five marbles in her large hand.

"And what's in the bag that you're so keen to protect?" Lane carried on, hoping Teensy wouldn't decide to beat the shit out of her. Lane wasn't small, but Teensy could snap her in half.

"None of your business." Wendy's voice was high-pitched.

"I told you—" Marbles scattered as Teensy stood up, all red-faced and clenched fists.

"Both of you, stop," Meg said, manoeuvring herself between Teensy and Lane. "I agree with Lane that Wendy knows more than she's letting on."

"She already said she doesn't," Teensy said and turned to Meg. "You should have more respect." But the anger had gone out of her, and Lane thought she probably wouldn't be pounded just yet. "Don't you think if Wendy knew something, she'd tell us? You think she'd just let us run around like headless chickens? Of course she wouldn't. She'd tell us what she knew. People are dying here."

"Okay, fine. Tell me about the Viking landings," Lane said to Wendy.

"What? Why?" Wendy asked.

"Well, this whole thing started when that treasure was found. And the chief zombie looks a little like a Viking, don't you think?" Tenuous, but Lane had a feeling.

"Why can't you just leave her alone? She's suffered enough. We all have," Teensy said.

"Why are you so quick to defend her? All I'm doing is asking her about the Viking landings," Lane snapped.

"What you're doing is harassing her. If Wendy knew something, she'd tell us." Teensy sat back down and spoke into the floor. "When my mom got the cancer, Wendy was the only one who kept on visiting her. Only one who came every week, right up until the end. All my mom's other so-called friends disappeared. Wendy's got integrity. If she knew something she thought could help us, she'd tell us. Isn't that right, Wendy?"

Wendy sighed. "I'll tell you what I know, but I don't see how it'll help us. What's happening here, this isn't normal. I don't know anything about *this*."

"Anything you can tell us might help." Meg came and sat at the table with Lane and Wendy.

"Well, back in 1006 or 1007—it's difficult to pinpoint exactly—Thorvold Eriksson was part of a Viking expedition to North America. There's no actual agreement among historians, but it's always been my personal belief he docked here in Provincetown." Wendy's eyes lit up, and her face became animated.

Lane thought Wendy would probably be a good teacher. "The Viking treasure those workmen found proved you were right."

"Exactly," Wendy said and favoured Lane with a smile. "For whatever reason, the treasure was buried here. Now, my guess is it was buried with a body. But the body wasn't dug up with the treasure. I think they stopped digging when they found the treasure. I wanted them to go down further, but they wouldn't. Goddamn Boston got involved and ordered everyone to stop immediately. Like we're ignorant bumpkins who can't tie our own shoes."

"Why would someone be buried with treasure?" Meg asked.

"It was a kind of Viking insurance policy. They believed that sometimes, a person who was particularly mean or greedy might come back from the dead to claim their worldly possessions or exact revenge on the living. To stop that from happening, they buried them with their belongings. There's a few Norse sagas written about it," Wendy said.

"Hang on a second." Teensy got up and came over to the table. "You're trying to say this big zombie dude is a dead Viking who wants his treasure back?"

"No, of course not. That's what I was saying before. I don't know anything about what's going on in Provincetown." Wendy gripped her bag tighter.

"Why not?" Lane asked. "Why can't it be a Viking zombie?"

"Draugr," Wendy corrected her. "Viking zombies are called draugr."

"You must have been dropped hard on your head when you were a baby," Teensy said to Lane. "You think some Viking zombie is roaming around Ptown looking for his treasure?"

"Well, what do you think it is?" Lane stood up. She was a head shorter than Teensy, but she wanted to be standing when Teensy decided to knock ten bells out of her.

"Government shit. Probably the army testing some biological agent. It got loose, and now everyone's turning into zombies," Teensy said.

"That doesn't sound any less insane than my theory," Lane said.

"*My* theory has plausibility." Teensy poked Lane in the chest. "Yours is just stupid."

"Don't poke me, Teensy." Lane felt her face heat. She'd had just about enough of Teensy Day.

"Or what?" Teensy asked and took a step closer.

"Lane. Teensy." Meg pushed herself in between them. "Would you both just cut it out? We're in trouble here, and the last thing we need is you two going at it. It doesn't really matter where the zombies came from. What matters is they're here and they want to eat us. We need to try to stay alive. Not fight amongst ourselves."

"It matters if it's one of these *draggers*," Lane said.

"Draugr," Wendy corrected her, shifting the accent on the word.

"Whatever. The point is, if it's a *draugr*, then we find the treasure and give it back. The draugr goes back to his grave. All's well that ends well."

"Not quite that simple," Wendy said. "According to my research, the Viking that may have been buried here would be Ivar Sigmarsson. I can't find any mention of him after Eriksson's boat arrives in Provincetown. If it is him, we'd all better hope Teensy's right about government experiments."

"Why?" Meg asked.

Wendy took a deep breath. "He was a nasty son of a bitch. He once burned a village in what's now England to the ground and slaughtered its inhabitants because his favourite dog ate some rotten meat there and died. He wasn't a forgiving man."

"Great," Lane said. "So he isn't keen on the English. Who is?"

"I'm serious. If what's going on *is* to do with Ivar Sigmarsson, we're in a lot of trouble. He won't go away just because he got his treasure back. He'll want revenge. All draugr do. They hate the living," Wendy said.

"I thought you said it wasn't to do with these draugr," Meg said.

"It isn't. But if it is…Oh, how would I know?" Wendy stood up suddenly and slid out of the booth. "How can anyone possibly know? This just isn't normal. It isn't right." She looked around. Her face was red and sweating.

"Wendy?" Meg reached out and squeezed her shoulder. "Wendy, it's okay."

"No, it isn't. Not at all." Wendy pulled away from Meg. "I need to use the bathroom."

"You want me to come with you?" Teensy asked.

"No, I need some time to myself. Just leave me alone. All of you, just leave me alone."

Wendy hurried out.

❖

"Well, what do you think?" Meg asked.

She was sitting at the table with Lane beside her and Teensy opposite with Lois asleep on her lap.

She watched Lane sigh and rub her face. Meg had the overwhelming urge to reach out and run her hand over Lane's broad back. Her hand twitched with the want.

"I still think it's the government," Teensy said.

"But zombies?" Meg asked.

"I wouldn't put anything past those assholes," Teensy replied and ran a hand over Lois's head. "Main thing is to get this little one out of here. It's been three hours now, and no one's come to rescue us. Those zombies will be back. I don't want to be here when they do. I think it's time to go to the harbour."

"Lane? What do you think? You've been very quiet." Meg bumped Lane gently with her shoulder.

"I agree. It's been too quiet. I still think Wendy knows more than she's letting on. There has to be some way to stop this thing," Lane said.

"What do you mean?" Teensy asked.

"Well, if these zombies are in Provincetown, there's nothing to say they won't get out and spread across the US. You saw how quick it happens. And presumably this chief zombie—Ivar Sigmarsson—is making new zombies out of living people. We need to do something."

Meg looked at Lane. At her earnest face. This was not the Lane she remembered. The Lane she knew only cared about partying and having a good time. Or maybe Meg had misjudged her completely. Was it possible she'd been so hung up on the fact Lane was rich—and she wasn't—that she'd blinded herself to who Lane really was? Did she have a huge chip on her shoulder like Lane said?

"We are doing something. Getting the fuck out of here

and telling the authorities in Boston. Let them call the army in. The navy. They'll blow these assholes to kingdom come," Teensy said.

"I thought you were convinced it was the government?" Meg said.

"I don't know what the hell it is, and neither do you. All I know is I want out of Provincetown, and I say we let the big boys handle it." Teensy stood up with Lois in her arms. "I'm going to get Wendy, and then we're leaving. You coming?"

Meg looked at Lane. "We should go with them, Lane."

When had she thrown her lot in with Lane? When had she started thinking of them as an *us*?

"Okay." Lane nodded. "It makes sense."

Chapter Eleven

 Outer Cape Echo
1 hour ago

Something very strange is happening in Provincetown. Reports having been coming in thick and fast about military vehicles spotted on Route 6. Are they on their way to the town, and if they are, why? Just what is happening over there? If you've heard anything, let us know in the comments below. In the meantime, our fearless reporters are on the case and bringing you all the breaking news out of the Cape.

523 Likes   *3 Comments*

Cory French: My mom lives over in Truro. She saw a bunch of military trucks heading towards Provincetown about an hour ago. Makes you wonder what the hell happened over there.

Ingrid Turner: I'd bet it's a military experiment gone wrong. Or aliens. I haven't been able to get a hold of my sister since last night. I just tried to drive over there, and the military are blocking all the roads into the town. Won't let anyone in.

Phil Greenwood: Me and some others are driving over there now. We're going to demand to know what's happening. It's not right they won't tell us. If you want to join us, we're meeting outside the beach cottages on Shore Road.

❖

It was full dark now. Across the water, lights twinkled, but in Provincetown, there were none. The only sound was the waves crashing against the shore. It had turned cold too, and Lane's hoodie did nothing to keep it out.

They'd agreed to walk along the beach as far as they could and to stay away from the roads. It seemed safer that way. All the same, Lane didn't mind admitting she was scared. Out here they were exposed and vulnerable. At least back in the Squealing Pig there was the illusion of safety. This was the right thing to do, though.

"It's choppy out there," Teensy whispered, dropping back to walk with Lane. She'd zipped Lois up inside her jacket, deciding it was better to carry her. Lois had her head buried in Teensy's neck. The child had barely spoken. Lane didn't blame her. If she was scared, she couldn't imagine what Lois must be feeling.

"But you think we can still get away on your boat?" Lane asked.

Teensy was quiet for a moment. "I don't think we have much other choice. Ordinarily I'd say no, but the alternative is…Well, I don't have to tell you."

Lane nodded. Everyone was aware of what the stakes were if they stayed. Lane still couldn't believe the authorities hadn't ridden into town yet. It seemed unlikely the outside world was still unaware what was happening here.

Maybe Teensy was right. Maybe it was some big government balls-up. Maybe they were discussing nuking Provincetown right now. All the more reason to get the fuck out of here. Thank God MacMillan Pier was only a short walk away.

"Okay, here it is," Teensy said and stopped. "We need to get back up onto the street and get to the dock via Standish."

"Sounds risky," Meg said.

Teensy shrugged. "No other way."

"All right. We move fast. I'll go first and scout the way," Lane said. "Teensy, you come up last."

"Last? Now hold on—" Teensy said.

"You're the only one who can operate the boat. And you have Lois. I'll go first," Lane said.

Teensy huffed, then nodded. "Makes sense."

"Not really," Meg said. "Lane, you don't know Provincetown well. I do. I should go first and scout the way."

"Absolutely not," Lane said.

"No way," Teensy replied at the same time.

"Don't go pulling the butch card on me now, ladies. It makes sense." Meg sounded tetchy.

"It's not a butch thing," Lane said.

"It's kind of a butch thing," Teensy said.

"You're both pissing me off. I know Provincetown, Lane doesn't. Having short hair isn't going to change that," Meg said.

"We'll go together, then," Lane said.

"Fine." Meg started off up the beach. "Teensy, Wendy. I'll flash the light on my cell phone twice if it's safe for you to come up."

"All right," Teensy said.

Wendy had barely said a word since they'd left the Pig. She was wrestling with something, and Lane hoped it was telling them the truth.

She opened her mouth to say something to Wendy, something reassuring. But she couldn't think of a thing to say, so she nodded instead and followed Meg.

❖

Meg led Lane to the bottom of the pier. In her mind she'd planned for them to climb up rather than cutting through the parking lot. The quickest route, of course, would have been to come out of the Pig and walk down Commercial. But for whatever reason, the zombies seemed to be staying away from the beach, so it had made sense to come this way.

But her original plan was going to be a problem now because there was no way Wendy and Lois were climbing up here. They'd have to go up past the Coffee Pot and cut down that way. They would still mostly avoid Commercial Street, but it was a risk all the same.

"What are we doing?" whispered Lane.

"Thinking," Meg whispered back.

"Oh, okay. Thinking about what?"

"Wendy and Lois are never going to be able to climb up here." Meg touched one of the wooden struts that held up MacMillan Pier. It was rough and cold under her hand. "We're going to need to go up there."

"Back onto Commercial?" Lane asked.

"Maybe not all the way, but at least to the end of the parking lot."

"Okay. Then that's what we'll do. We'd better hurry. It's getting darker—if that's possible."

Meg looked up at the sky. Thick cloud blanketed it as though it was the middle of winter. Lane was right. It was getting darker. Meg was also having reservations about their chances out on the ocean. The swell looked rough and unforgiving. But the alternative was being eaten alive in Provincetown.

"Let's go," Meg said.

Lane drew alongside her as they walked up between the

buildings. Meg glanced at her. Lane's jaw was tight, and her usually grinning mouth was set in grim determination. She clutched a hammer in one hand, and Meg had no doubt Lane would use it to defend both of them. The thought made her feel a little less afraid. Lane was no coward—she'd proved that today—and Meg felt ashamed for ever thinking she was.

Before she could think about it, Meg reached out and squeezed Lane's shoulder. "Thank you," she said.

Lane turned at her and smiled. "What for?"

"For everything. I...I'm glad you're here, Lane. I'm not sure I would have made it this far without you," Meg said. She needed to say it. Suddenly, it seemed as though time was very short, and she had a lot of things to say to Lane. Most of them started with sorry. She wished they had more time.

"Of course you would have made it this far. Just minus the eye candy," Lane said and winked.

Meg laughed and rolled her eyes. "Still the same old Lane," she said.

"No." Lane stopped abruptly and reached for Meg's free hand with hers. "No, I don't think I am. Not at all. I have a lot of things to say to you, Meg. I just wish we had more time."

"When this is over, okay? We'll talk. Properly talk, when this is over and we're safe." Meg squeezed Lane's hand.

Lane nodded. "Yeah."

And then, all hell broke loose.

❖

At the sound of the first scream, Lane turned in the direction of the beach. In the distance, she saw five or six zombies rushing towards Teensy, Wendy, and Lois. There were more further up the beach.

"Jesus fucking Christ," she whispered and gripped Meg's hand.

A couple of the quickest zombies had already reached the others, and Teensy was doing her best to fight them off.

"Come on," Lane said and began to run. Meg came willingly.

Lane was under no illusion that any of them was making it out of this alive, but she couldn't leave her friends to die alone. They'd do what they could.

Teensy must have said something to Lois and Wendy because they began to run towards her and Meg.

"Don't you dare come down here, Lane. I mean it—I'll kick your ass," Teensy bellowed from where she stood on the beach.

"We aren't leaving you," Meg cried, just as Lois and Wendy reached them.

Lane let go of Meg's hand. "Meg, get them to safety. I'll help Teensy."

"Lane, I swear to God if you come down here—" Teensy's words were cut off as she launched a zombie away from her and into the sea. "I'm already bit. I'll hold 'em off, but you run."

Lane could see the rest of the zombies getting closer. They were almost upon Teensy. She took another step towards Teensy.

"Don't you fucking dare, you tea-drinking, monarch-loving son of a bitch," Teensy screamed. "*Dawn's Crack.* Get to that when you can, but for now get out of here."

Teensy caught another zombie around the head with her hammer. The horde was almost upon her.

"Okay," Lane shouted. "Okay." She wiped the tears falling from her cheeks.

The zombies stumbled and fell as they made their way up the beach in huge numbers. Teensy had no chance at all. Lane took one look back as they ran to Commercial Street and wished she hadn't. Teensy was gone. Lost beneath a writhing mass of the walking dead.

Teensy had saved all their lives by giving up her own.

Chapter Twelve

 Outer Cape Echo
10 minutes ago

BREAKING NEWS: You heard it here first. Something strange is happening in Provincetown. All day long military personnel have been flooding into the Outer Cape. Reports from eyewitnesses say authorities have quarantined the tiny town. All roads are closed out of Truro, and there's talk that the cordon may extend even further as authorities get to grips with what's going on.

So far, they've been tight-lipped about what's happening in Provincetown, but sources have pointed towards a terrorist incident which may have killed most of the inhabitants.

Anyone making their way to the area should be warned that there are military patrols coming down hard on anyone who tries to get past the quarantine. Several people have already been placed under arrest. More to follow as we get information.

45k Likes   *6 Comments*

Paul Thomas: It's zombies and I know this for a fact.

Marie Collins: Bullshit. My cousin is in the National Guard and nobody will tell them anything, but she's seen people going in and out of there in those space suits with the masks. Everyone's saying it's some kind of chemical spill.

Paul Thomas: It's zombies. Marie, you're an idiot.

Michael Fish: Paul, are you related to **Dolores Cab** by any chance?

Paul Thomas: *[post deleted by moderator]*

Connie Smith: We'll take that as a yes. Zombies. How ridiculous.

❖

Meg watched as Lane nailed up boards on the back door of the Squealing Pig. Full dark had fallen, and there was no way they were getting out of town now. They'd have to wait until morning.

Since they got back here, Lane had been totally silent. Lois had curled up on a bench in the bar under a pile of their coats with her eyes squeezed shut, though Meg knew she wasn't sleeping. Wendy was hunched over on a chair with her bag clutched tightly to her chest. They were in a bad way, their little gang.

Meg thought about Teensy and what she'd done for them. Meg wondered if she had it in her to give her life for others. That was the ultimate bravery, wasn't it? Dying so that other people might live. Teensy hadn't even hesitated. She knew what was going to happen to her, and she hadn't even paused to think about it.

Meg looked over at Wendy again. How could she just sit there like that? She hadn't said a word since they got back. She'd been in a relationship with Teensy, for Christ's sake.

Meg knew she had the treasure in that bag, but she wouldn't give it up. Not even for Teensy. Instead, she was still pretending like she didn't know anything about what was going on in Provincetown.

Meg couldn't help thinking all of this was on her. True, Wendy hadn't been the one to dig up the treasure, and if she was right about the Norse legends, then Ptown was screwed as soon as the work crew removed the treasure from Winthrop Street. But if Wendy knew—or at least suspected—that was why all this happened, why wouldn't she just say so?

Because then she'd have to hand over the treasure and put it back in this Ivar Sigmarsson's grave like Lane wanted. For whatever reason, Wendy didn't want to give it up.

Meg tried to be charitable. After all, their current situation might have nothing to do with Vikings—the whole thing sounded totally far-fetched. A government experiment gone wrong did sound much more likely, but even so Wendy wasn't even willing to contemplate it.

And now, Teensy was dead. Or worse than dead. It wasn't fair. Meg hadn't exactly been close with Teensy, but she'd liked her. They'd had a drink together more than a few times. Teensy hadn't deserved to die, and if Meg found out Wendy could have prevented it, she'd kill Wendy herself.

Meg tracked Lane as she went behind the bar and poured herself a drink. A big one. Meg guessed she deserved it. Even Lois probably deserved a large Scotch. That kid was going to be messed up for life after this.

"I'll have one too," Meg said.

Lane nodded and got another glass. "Water?"

"No. Thank you. I consider watering down good Scotch a crime," Meg said.

"I don't think this is good Scotch, Meg." Lane sniffed it and wrinkled her nose. "I'm not sure if this is even whisky."

"It doesn't matter. As long as it takes the edge off," Meg said.

"Yeah. It might do that." Lane brought the drinks and the bottle over to the table Meg was at and sat down.

"How are you holding up?" Lane asked before she took a hefty swig of whatever was in the glass.

Meg did the same. Brandy. Cheap brandy. "I'm not sure. I mean, I'm functioning. You know, walking, talking, drinking shitty booze. Beyond that, I just can't say. What about you?"

Lane shrugged. "I feel like I'm in a waking nightmare. Or a video game."

"You know Wendy has that Viking zombie's treasure, right? In her bag," Meg whispered.

"Yeah. I know. I've been thinking about that. I mean, say it is this zombie. He's had his treasure nicked, or whatever. Surely if we give it back, he'll leave us alone. Won't he?"

"I don't know. I mean, the whole thing sounds crazy. But Wendy is refusing to let us look in her bag, and short of forcing her to give it to us, what can we do?" Meg asked.

"Convince her to give us the bag. I can go to his burial place or whatever it's called, leave the treasure there, and hopefully he'll go away," Lane said.

"And if he doesn't? And you end up getting killed?" Meg felt sick at the thought of Lane going back out there.

"Then at least we tried. Have you got any better ideas?" Lane drank the rest of her brandy and shivered. "God, that's horrible."

"You want another?" Meg asked.

"Sure." Lane picked up the bottle and poured them another.

"The authorities must know what's going on by now, right?" Meg said.

"You'd think so, but if they do, where are they?"

"I don't know. But it seems ridiculous to think they have no idea what's happening here," Meg said.

"Unless these zombies got out and are taking over the whole country," Lane said.

"Yeah, there is that. Way to lighten the mood, Lane."

Lane smiled. "Sorry, is that what we were doing?"

Meg sighed. "No. We were trying to figure a way out of this mess. I vote we make Wendy give us her bag."

"We can't do that. We should try to talk her round first," Lane said.

"Lane, for Christ's sake. She's had a ton of opportunities to give it up, but she won't. For whatever reason, she won't. She is not going to let us just have that bag."

"So we take it? What if she resists? Do we fight her? Hit her?" Lane asked.

"No. Maybe? I don't know. All I know is that there's a good chance we're in this mess because of her. If we are, she's responsible for a lot of shit and doesn't deserve any kindness."

"Come on, Meg. She wasn't to know this would happen," Lane said.

"Right, but she must have figured it out pretty quickly once people started turning into fucking zombies," Meg said, struggling to keep her voice to a whisper. "Why are you defending her?"

"I'm not. I just don't think this is entirely her fault. She wasn't to know. Let's talk to her first. See what she says," Lane said.

"Fine." Meg nodded and looked over to the table where Wendy had been sitting. "She's gone."

"What?" Lane looked round too. "She can't have gotten far."

Meg glanced over to the pile of coats covering Lois. "Maybe she just went to the bathroom."

Lane walked down to the back of the bar where the bathrooms were. Meg followed close behind.

Lane knocked on the door. "Wendy? Are you in there?"

"Leave me alone. Both of you," came Wendy's muffled response.

"We just want to talk to you, Wendy. About your bag," Meg said.

"I know what you want. You want my treasure. Well, you can't have it."

Meg looked at Lane. "Can you kick the door in?" she whispered.

Lane looked shocked. "No. We aren't kicking in any doors. She has to come out sometime."

"And until then, we just wait out here?" Meg asked.

"Wendy?" Lane spoke to the door. "No one is trying to take your treasure. We just want to talk to you. Work out if giving him back the stuff will make all this stop."

"It won't. And you're crazy. Viking zombies? Can you hear yourself?" Wendy said. Her voice was shrill, and even through the door Meg could tell Wendy was on the edge.

"You said yourself, draugr get the arse when someone takes their stuff." Lane continued to try to reason with Wendy, which astounded Meg. Lane was kind of amazing in a crisis. "Could we not just give it back to him?" Lane asked.

"No. Don't be stupid. This situation is an experiment, or a chemical spill. *Not* zombies," Wendy replied.

Lane leaned her head against the door and Meg felt sorry for her.

"Look, Wendy," Meg joined in. "Get out here. We can put the treasure back where it was found, and if that doesn't work, then you can have it back. How does that sound?"

"I already told you—no. You wouldn't be doing this if

Teensy was here. Do you know how long I've spent studying and writing papers and trying to convince people that Vikings landed in Provincetown?"

Lane looked at Meg and shrugged. "No. But—"

"Twenty years. And now that I have proof, now that I can show all those people who told me I was wasting my time, they want to take it all off me. Send it to Boston. What is Boston going to do with it that I won't? This treasure belongs here in Provincetown. With me."

Lane looked at Meg and shook her head. Meg nodded. There was no point in trying to talk to Wendy.

But like Lane said, she'd have to come out sometime. And when she did, she and Lane would take the bag. They wouldn't hurt her, but they would take the bag.

"What shall we do? Go back in the bar?" Lane asked.

"No point waiting out here. She's not going anywhere. Only one way out, and all the doors are barred. We'll hear her trying to get out," Meg said.

"I don't think she'd go out there by herself anyway. She's terrified," Lane said.

Meg walked back to the table and picked up their glasses. "I don't think we should have any more of this."

"I agree. We should probably eat, though. Is there food in the kitchen?"

"Sure. Tons of it. Sandwiches again?" Meg asked.

"Yeah. We were lucky to get back here without running into more of them, and I don't want the smell attracting them to us," Lane said.

"There's still some cold cuts and cheeses. And another loaf of bread out back."

"Sounds good. Lois?" Lane gently shook Lois's shoulder. "You hungry?"

The coats moved and Lois stuck her head out. "No," she said.

"You should try to eat something even if you don't feel like it, honey," Meg said.

"I don't want anything. I just want to go to sleep," Lois said and stuck her head back under the coats.

Meg didn't blame her. If she had her way, she'd probably bury herself under a pile of coats and not come out either. But she couldn't. It was up to her and Lane to get them out of this mess.

Right now, food sounded good. Normal, even. The whole town had gone crazy in a few short hours. Meg found it hard to believe that just this morning she was thinking about how to get rid of Lane. Now, she'd never been so grateful for anyone in her life. Lane had proved herself to be all the things Meg accused her of being deficient in. Solid, reliable, brave. Selfless. So what did that make Meg? How had she misjudged Lane so badly?

Meg knew she wasn't a bad judge of character. So what was it about Lane that made Meg judge her so harshly? As she watched Lane inspect the boards covering the doors and windows, Meg thought she might know, and it made her ashamed.

All her life, she'd walked around with a chip on her shoulder about wealth. Told herself she was better than those people who had it handed to them on a plate. She'd been attracted to Lane and despised her at the same time because of her privilege. Meg admitted to herself she'd been cruel. She'd treated Lane like nothing more than a fling and then dropped her without care—maybe she'd planned it all along subconsciously. Or maybe that was too harsh.

The truth was, she'd liked Lane. Maybe even been halfway

in love with her. Perhaps that had scared her too. Either way, she'd dropped her like a sack of potatoes and then been angry when Lane hadn't come running after her. And then, Lane did come running.

And Meg had been cruel.

Meg squeezed her eyes shut and rubbed her temples. She'd been so cruel.

"What's up?"

Meg jumped when Lane touched her shoulder.

"Sorry. I didn't mean to make you jump." Lane sat down next to her. "Teensy did a good job on the boards. But there's a couple loose. I'll sort them out in a bit."

"Lane, we need to talk," Meg said. The urge to do it now was overwhelming.

"Okay. What about?" Lane asked.

"Us."

"Us? Is this really the right time?" Lane asked.

"Probably not, but when else? There's things I need to say to you. And I…they can't wait," Meg said.

Lane nodded. "Is there somewhere we can go? I don't want to do it in front of Lois."

"Sure. I have a little office off the kitchen." Meg stood.

"But what about Wendy? She's still in the bathroom."

"Where's she going to go? Everything's boarded up. Plus, she's terrified. She won't leave the bar."

"Okay." Lane stood too.

Meg felt equal parts dread and relief. She needed to say things, so many things. And Lane was allowing her to in a way she hadn't done for Lane. Another thing to feel guilt for.

❖

Lane followed Meg into the office. It was a tight fit. Lane motioned for Meg to take the only chair while she perched on the edge of the desk.

"Okay," Meg said, and Lane watched her take a deep breath. "I've been an asshole to you."

Lane stayed silent. She couldn't argue.

"A total asshole. And not just here, in Ptown. In London too. I treated you badly, and Lane, I am so, so sorry. Please, forgive me."

Lane was at a loss for words. She stared at Meg. This wasn't what she'd been expecting. "Of course I forgive you," Lane said. "And I'm sorry for—"

"No." Meg held up a hand. "No, this is all on me. You have nothing to be sorry for."

"I do, Meg. I've been most of the things you said I was. Childish, aimless. I never understood why you wanted to work so hard when I could just buy you what you wanted. I think I do now."

"You do?" Meg asked.

"Yes. Today has been a steep learning curve for me. I never meant to try to buy you, Meg."

"I know. I have a chip on my shoulder about the size of the Cape. I build walls and push people away. I'm terrified of commitment, and I use my bar as a reason not to get close to anyone—God, I sound like Dr. Phil." Meg laughed. "I guess I never wanted to think about all this stuff before, Lane. But almost dying and being trapped in a bar while zombies rampage outside can kind of put things into perspective. When I saw you at Joanne's, I panicked. No one's ever come halfway around the world for me before."

Lane nodded. It was hard to speak around the lump in her throat. "I did fight for you back in London too, you know."

"What do you mean?"

"After the pub, after you dumped me." Lane looked up at Meg's face. God, she loved her. "I went to your flat."

❖

"*Just get over it.*"

Lane looked up from her beer and into the face of her closest friend. "It's not that easy."

Sophia rolled her eyes. "What I don't understand is why you're so upset. You told me you weren't even that bothered."

"I lied." Lane pushed the pint away. She'd spent the last week in a drunken stupor, and the smell of booze was starting to turn her stomach.

"What do you mean?" Sophia asked and pulled Lane's pint over to her side of the table. She'd drink literally anything.

"I mean, I lied. I pretended I didn't care because...I suppose my pride was wounded. I don't know. The point is, Sophia, I think I love her."

"Oh, for God's sake." Sophia rolled her eyes. "I thought we agreed we weren't ever falling in love. We made a pact."

Lane looked up at her friend and smiled. "We were seven."

"So? We swore on Celine Dion."

"No, you swore on Celine Dion. I went along with it because...because..."

"Because that's what you always do, Lane. Anything for an easy life. Anything to avoid making your own decisions and risking hurting somebody's feelings," Sophia said.

"Yeah." Lane sighed. "And look where it's gotten me."

"You're a great artist, you know," Sophia said. "I always thought your parents were wrong to stop you pursuing that."

"What's that got to do with this?" Lane asked.

"It's part of the point I'm making about you doing what you're told to avoid rocking the boat."

"Oh." Lane felt a little exposed. She and Sophia rarely talked like this. "They didn't stop me, exactly," Lane said.

"As good as. Threw a load of money at you and told you to forget about it. And you went along with it because—"

"That's what I do," Lane finished. "I'm weak."

"You aren't at all." Sophia reached for her hand and held it. "You're just so used to doing what your family tell you because the alternative is losing the money they chuck at you. They've got you over a barrel. Don't worry—I'm in the same boat."

"I don't want to live like that any more." The realization hit Lane like an oar off a rowing boat. "I'm so sick of being me."

"There's absolutely nothing wrong with you," Sophia said.

"I'm entitled."

Sophia rolled her eyes. "We all are."

"I'm spoiled, I'm lazy. It's no wonder Meg dumped me," Lane said.

"Meg dumped you for reasons that are her own, and that's not on you, Lane. As much as I hate to compliment you, you're one of the nicest people I know. You're loyal, which is rare in our social circle, and you're accepting. Again, also rare in our circle."

"It's not enough," Lane said.

"What do you mean?" Sophia asked.

"I'm not sure. For the last year I've been restless. I can't explain it except to say that I feel as though there's something more I'm supposed to do with my life. We're so aimless, Sophia. So lost."

Lane saw Sophia bristle at that. "Well, I'm happy with my life. I may not have a job, but I do charity stuff and—"

"I wasn't having a go. I'm sorry—I didn't mean to insult you. I just meant that I'm not *happy. I'm not content. In all honesty, I'm fucking miserable." There. She'd said it. Out loud. She was miserable and had been for years. No amount of money was going to change it.*

"Then do something about it. Go and get your girl," Sophia said.

"You know, I think I will." Lane laughed, and suddenly she felt lighter. She'd made a decision for herself, for her happiness. She stood up.

"Where are you going?" Sophia asked.

"To get Meg back."

"What, now?"

"Why wait?" Lane asked.

Sophia shrugged. "Fair enough. Want a lift?"

"That would be great," Lane said.

❖

"But you didn't come and get me back," Meg said.

"I did. I went to your flat, but your roommate said you'd gone. Back to America," Lane said.

"I'm sorry." Meg squeezed Lane's shoulder. She'd had no idea. Her roommate never mentioned it when she emailed to settle the last of the bills. They weren't close, though.

"It's not your fault. I left it too long. I suppose I didn't know you were planning on leaving so soon. I thought you were in London for longer. But I must have misunderstood."

"No, I'd planned to be. Two days after I ended things with you, my mom called. She told me my brother was in a car wreck. I went home and spent all the money I'd saved to open the bar on his medical bills. No National Health Service in the US."

"I had no idea. I'm sorry," Lane said. "You could have asked me for help, you know."

"Seriously? After I'd just dumped you? Besides, I'm not good at doing that. It's too hard, for too many reasons."

Lane nodded. "I know. Must be lonely though."

"You get used to it," Meg said and tried not to think about how right Lane was.

All she did was work and sleep and dream about her bar. She had no real friends, just customers from the Pig. She couldn't remember the last time she'd taken a vacation or spent money on something. Every penny went in the bank. She'd barely lived a life at thirty-two years old, and now it might end here in Provincetown. The only thing she'd have to show for it was thirteen thousand dollars.

Truth was, she didn't know if she and Lane had any kind of future together, but she realized now, all her assumptions about Lane were wrong. Badly wrong. And if Lane wasn't the person Meg had thought she was and was, in fact, everything Meg wanted, what did that mean?

Meg looked up at Lane. She'd never realized before what kind eyes Lane had. Warm and welcoming and open. She rose up slightly from the chair and watched Lane's eyes widen in surprise.

"Meg, are you—"

"Just shut up and kiss me, Lane."

Lane obliged, and the feel of her lips on Meg's was incredible. Meg remembered those kisses. How gentle Lane could be. How soft her lips were.

Meg deepened the kiss, dipped her tongue inside Lane's mouth, and heard Lane groan. Then Lane took control of the kiss. Meg felt herself being lifted out of the chair and turned around so that her back was to the desk. Lane stood between her legs and pressed close.

Their kiss became more demanding, and Lane's arms came around her waist, slid down her hips, and grasped her ass. Lane pulled Meg tight against her, and Meg tilted her pelvis into Lane's.

Then Lane's hands were on her breasts over her shirt. Lane's thumbs brushed over her nipples, and it was Meg's turn to groan. Meg reached down and pushed her hands beneath Lane's jeans. She slid her hands inside Lane's underwear and ran her fingernails over Lane's ass.

"Shit." Lane groaned.

In one swift movement, Lane reached beneath Meg's shirt and unhooked her bra, slid the straps down. She pushed Meg's shirt up and pulled Meg's nipple in her mouth. Meg held Lane's head against her breast and leaned in to her. She'd forgotten how good Lane's mouth felt.

Lane moved to the other breast, and at the same time Meg felt Lane's fingers on her jeans. Were they really going to do this? Have sex right here? Was it a good idea? And not just because of the whole zombie apocalypse thing. Meg didn't want to hurt Lane again. Her emotions were all over the place. Did she want to be with Lane? Did it matter? The chances of them making it out of this alive weren't good.

Now Lane's fingers were inside Meg's underwear, and all thought and reason went out the window.

Meg helped Lane pull down her panties, impatient now. She spread her legs as much as she could with her pants around her ankles and leaned back on the desk.

Meg sighed when Lane's fingers eased inside her. It had been so long since she'd let someone touch her like this. The last person had been Lane, she realized.

"You okay? Should I stop?" Lane asked, obviously sensing her start.

"No, no, don't stop." Meg pulled Lane close and kissed her.

Lane's fingers began to move inside Meg, and when Lane thrust her hips against them, Meg groaned at the sensation. Meg tightened her arms around Lane's neck, kicked one leg out of her jeans, and wrapped her legs around Lane's waist. It felt so good. Sex with Lane had always been good. The best.

Lane's movements sped up, fingers curling inside her to stroke her G-spot. Meg knew she wouldn't come like this, but it felt incredible all the same. Lane must have remembered too because she pulled back and out of Meg and dropped to her knees.

Lane slid one of Meg's legs out of her jeans and panties and parted her legs further.

"Is this okay?" Lane asked.

Meg nodded. "Yes. Please, Lane."

And then Lane's mouth was on her, and Meg closed her eyes and let her head drop back. She reached out and held Lane's head to her as she moved her hips against Lane's mouth. Within moments she was coming. The orgasm washed over her and ran right through her. Meg felt boneless and drowsy and better than she had in months.

She reached down and lifted Lane's head where it rested on her thigh. "I forgot how good you were at that," Meg said.

Lane smiled. "I forgot how much I liked doing it with you."

"Come up here," Meg said.

Lane stood and Meg wrapped her in a hug. "That was fast, even for you."

"It's been a long time." Meg laughed. "Actually, you were my last."

Lane pulled back and away from her. "Are you serious?"

Meg nodded. "I wouldn't lie. I take it that I'm not your last." She knew she had no right, but Meg was a little stung at the thought of Lane being with other women. A little stung and a lot jealous. She had no right, but she couldn't help how she felt.

"Actually, you are," Lane said. "I told you—I love you. I wasn't interested in anyone else."

Meg felt a surge of warmth somewhere dangerously close to her heart. What was she doing? This was the worst possible time to be getting involved in all the Lane stuff again. Dragging up the old feelings.

"We can talk about us when this is all over," Meg said. "I just don't think now is the right time."

"We just had sex," Lane said, and Meg could see the hurt in her eyes. Great. She'd done it again.

"I know, and it was great. But I think we need to focus on getting out of here. We've been away from the others for too long already." Meg started to stand, and Lane backed off. She pulled up her underwear and her pants.

"Fine. Whatever, Meg," Lane said.

"Lane, wait. I'm not trying—"

"It doesn't matter. You're right, we should get back to the others."

Lane walked out of the office before Meg could say any more.

Meg shut her eyes. She rubbed her forehead. What the hell was wrong with her? Once again, she'd acted like a total bitch to Lane.

Despite everything she'd realized about life being short and Lane not being the person she'd thought she was, Meg still couldn't allow herself to let Lane in. Once again, she'd panicked at the thought of lowering her walls, and once again she'd hurt Lane. How many times was she going to do that before Lane had enough? Meg wasn't a stupid woman, so why was she repeating the same mistakes? It was time for that to stop.

This time, she wouldn't leave it. They did need to talk. "Lane," Meg called. She walked back into the bar. Lane was standing by the bench where Lois slept.

"She's gone," Lane said.

"What? Who?" Meg moved to stand beside her.

"Lois. She's gone," Lane said again.

"Maybe she's in the bathroom." Meg swallowed down the panic.

"I don't think so. Look, some of the boards have been moved from the window. The loose ones. I think she's gone."

CHAPTER THIRTEEN

 Outer Cape Echo
15 minutes ago

BREAKING: Word coming out of the Outer Cape is that there's a siege in Provincetown. Heavy machine gun fire and loud explosions could be heard coming from the vicinity of the seaside town. Officials are keeping tight-lipped, but the word is the army has mounted some kind of operation. As we reported earlier in the day, large numbers of military vehicles were spotted making their way along Route 6. Just what is going on over there? If you know, tell us in the comments below.

---

421 Likes   *4 Comments*

Mike Finkel: Terrorists. It's always terrorists.

Jane Birch: My niece who lives over in Provincetown hasn't been able to get back in. She got a call from her father, who told her to stay out. He says he's boarded up his house and he's just waiting it out. He's got Alzheimer's, so I don't know if he's a reliable witness, but my niece said he was talking about zombies.

Grant Richardson: That's the biggest load of crap I ever heard. Zombies? Come on.

Dale White: I heard it's zombies too from my cousin who lives down that way. He said he saw someone chewing on a body like it was a juicy burger. I'm staying up in Hyannis until this blows over.

❖

When Lane checked the bathrooms, she knew with certainty they were both gone. Lois and Wendy. What the hell was Wendy thinking? Fair enough, she wanted to keep the Viking treasure for herself, but why take Lois too?

"She took Lois because she knows we'll go after her. Lois is a bargaining chip," Meg said.

"Surely not. How do you know that?" Lane asked.

"Because there's no reason she'd take a little kid with her if she wants to get out of Provincetown with the treasure. No reason except she knows we'll come after her, and Lois is her insurance. She knows we'll take Lois and not the treasure if it comes down to it."

"That's fucking cold," Lane said. "Maybe she thought she was helping Lois by taking her?"

Meg shook her head. "No, she wants that treasure and she knows we want it too—for different reasons. She thinks we'll let her keep it in return for Lois."

"I don't understand. Wendy didn't strike me as a bad person. Why would she do this?" Lane asked.

"Who knows? Maybe there's something about that treasure? If a Viking is willing to rise from the dead to get it back, it must be special," Meg said.

"But it doesn't make sense. I thought she was the kindly

local historian? When did she turn into such a psycho?" Lane asked.

"I don't know. I never knew Wendy all that well. I always got the sense she felt like she was better than everyone else. But maybe that was unfounded—I'm clearly not the best judge of character, am I?"

"So why is she doing this? I mean, Teensy was her friend. They were together. It seems odd that she wouldn't do everything to help us get out of this situation. Why hoard the treasure? Why take Lois?"

"I told you, Lane, I don't know. Maybe she got so caught up in her work that she lost her way. She's been here for years plugging away, trying to make something of her career, with all her exhibitions and papers. Perhaps this treasure was just too good to resist. It proves out her years of research, and it's worth a ton of money."

"You sound like you know a lot about her, for someone who says she doesn't know Wendy at all," Lane said.

"I just know what it's like to want something so badly that you lose sight of what's important," Meg said.

Lane could see Meg thought she'd said too much. A crack in her wall. And Lane got a glimpse of the regret Meg felt. Or maybe that was just Lane's wishful thinking. Meg had tuned her out as quickly as she'd let her in back in the office. Classic Meg move. It frustrated Lane and made her sad at the same time. Since they'd been in the Pig, Lane had sensed a thawing in Meg. But maybe that was only wishful thinking too.

Either way, they didn't have time to talk about their relationship right now. With luck, there would be a later. Meg sighed and Lane couldn't help herself. She reached out and stroked Meg's cheek.

"Yeah, I guess you do know what it's like," Lane said.

Then, before Meg could say anything else, she changed the subject. "Okay. Where would she go? The harbour?"

"Maybe. I guess she might try. I know she can sail a boat."

"But it's so risky. We didn't make it, and we had Teensy with us," Lane said.

"She's desperate. She's willing to die to keep hold of the treasure. And let Lois die too," Meg said. "I feel awful. While we were in there having sex, Wendy was taking Lois."

"I know. Meg, we have to get her back," Lane said.

"Yes. We have to go back out there. It's dark now—maybe that'll give us some kind of cover," Meg said.

"Maybe." Lane picked up her bag. She took out the hammer and handed it to Meg.

"Lane?" Meg said. "Whatever happens out there, Lois is our priority. If it's a choice between me and her, I want you to pick her." Meg tested the weight of the hammer in her hand, and it felt good. Solid. Heavy.

Lane nodded. "Same for me. We get Lois out of here. And we get that treasure. I think it's the key. I think it's what will put an end to this. Wendy said it herself—these draugr things want their treasure. If we can give it back, maybe it'll go away."

"I don't know if it's that simple, but it's certainly worth a shot," Meg said.

"It's the only one we have. Doesn't look as if the military are going to help us. Maybe the zombies already got out of Ptown," Lane said.

Shit, what was she saying? Where the zombies might have spread to didn't bear thinking about, and it was the last thing they needed distracting them right now. "Sorry. Killing the mood again."

Meg laughed and Lane smiled. She liked it when Meg laughed. "Don't worry about it. Ready to go?"

Lane nodded. She was as ready as she'd ever be. And how ready could you ever be to face a horde of flesh-eating zombies?

Lane watched as Meg pulled more boards loose so they could fit through.

❖

Outside, a bitter wind had kicked up. It was already full dark even though it wasn't yet six p.m. A newspaper twisted and flipped and danced its way down the deserted street. Meg was struck by how quiet it was. There should be people crowding the sidewalks and spilling out from the bars and restaurants. Instead, the place was empty. At least there weren't a bunch of zombies waiting for them.

This time, they didn't see any point in heading for the beach. Last time had shown them the zombies would eventually head down there, and at least up on Commercial there were more places to run and hide. On the beach they'd be trapped— just like Teensy was. Meg tried not to think about that. She thought that last image of Teensy being buried by a mass of swarming, biting bodies would stay with her for a long time.

"Stop," Lane whispered, and Meg realized she hadn't been paying attention.

Good work, she told herself. *Great way to get yourself killed.*

"What is it?" Meg asked.

"I can hear something. From there." Lane pointed at an alley to the right of them. "We should duck down here."

Lane and Meg moved behind a dumpster sitting in the alley next to them. Good thing about Provincetown—lots of alleys.

They crouched down and waited. Soon, they heard the

shuffling and the groaning that seemed to signal a zombie was nearby. Meg chanced a look around the side of the dumpster. Sure enough, there it was, shuffling down the street with a weird aimless determination. Like it was heading somewhere but didn't exactly know where. Who knew, maybe they still retained some of who they had been, and this zombie was heading to a home it dimly remembered.

They waited until it shuffled past, changed its mind, shuffled back, and headed up Freeman Street.

"Let's go," Lane whispered.

When they got to the parking lot at MacMillan Pier, Meg couldn't avoid looking left to where Teensy had died. It was too far away, but Meg swore she could see a dark pool of blood soaking into the sand.

They made slow progress, ducking behind cars and weaving their way towards the pier. Once they were on it, there would be no real options for escape should the zombies turn up. Really, the water would be their only out, and looking at it, Meg wasn't sure they'd survive that either. But drowning beat being eaten to death and coming back as one of *them*.

Suddenly, Meg heard a scream. It came from Commercial. "You hear that?" she asked Lane.

"Yeah. Might be Wendy," Lane said.

"It could be."

The scream came again, followed by someone calling for help. Definitely Wendy. Which meant she was alive. Which meant there was a good chance Lois was too.

"Let's go," Lane said and made a break for it.

Meg followed. Jesus, Lane was fast. Meg couldn't remember the last time she'd done any exercise. She was certainly paying for it now. She thought about promising the universe to do better if they survived, but…nah. If she got out of this alive, she'd probably still not do any exercise, truth be told.

Meg's lungs burned and so did her legs. She half expected to turn on to Commercial and see Ivar Sigmarsson blowing blue fire out of his mouth, but it was just the usual horde of twenty or thirty zombies.

Wendy and Lois were up on a car roof. Meg noticed the zombies were having trouble climbing, and that was something to bear in mind.

The zombies hadn't seen her and Lane yet, and maybe they could make that work.

"Lane, you hide. I'll make a ton of noise and try and make them follow me. That should give you time to get Wendy and Lois."

"No—"

"That bar there?" She pointed to the building on the corner by the car. "It's the Governor Bradford. You can hide in there. I'll circle back and find you."

"Meg, no."

"It's the only way."

"Then let me lead them off," Lane said.

"We don't have time for this. I know Provincetown. I know where I'm going, and you don't."

"But, Meg—"

Meg kissed her. It was all she could think to do. She didn't have the words to tell Lane how she felt about her, and even if she did, there wasn't time. She kissed her hard. Bruised her lips, probably. Then Meg stepped back, waited for Lane to take cover, and screamed at the top of her lungs.

❖

At the sound of Meg's warlike cry, Lane jumped up from where she'd been hiding and rushed up the street.

As Meg had hoped, the zombies turned and took off after her on a cacophony of groans. Lane didn't have time to follow her progress down the street. She felt sick and proud and terrified for Meg. She didn't have time for any of those feelings, though.

Once the last of the zombies had gone, Lane approached the car.

"Quickly," she said and held her arms out for Lois, who jumped into them. "You okay? Not hurt, not bitten?" she asked.

"No." Lois shook her head.

Lane put her down and focussed her attention on Wendy. "Here." She held out her hand. "Wendy, hurry up. We don't have time for this," Lane said.

"You're going to take the treasure." Wendy still didn't move.

"We can talk about that later. Meg just risked her life for you. Get down."

Wendy snorted. "No, she risked her life for her." She nodded at Lois. "If it had just been me, you'd have left me for dead."

Lane couldn't argue. "Which is the reason you took Lois. Either way, you're not dead thanks to Meg."

"If I come down, you're going to take it from me," Wendy said.

They really didn't have time for this. "No one's taking anything."

"I heard you talking, back at the Squealing Pig," Wendy said.

"Wendy, what—" Lane stopped dead in her tracks when Wendy pulled out a gun. "What the fuck are you doing?"

"Insurance. You won't mess with me while I've got this,"

Wendy said. "Now step back. We're getting out of here on *Dawn's Crack*. And you're going to get us there."

"No way," Lane said.

"Yes, you are. It's where we were headed until we got chased into a store by a bunch of *them*."

"Wendy, think about what you're doing. Is it really worth all this? For some jewellery?"

"It's not just jewellery. It's proof. Proof I was right. Proof of everything I've been working on for so many years. They won't laugh at me now. When I go to conferences, they'll treat me with the respect I deserve. I'm not burying it all over again for your stupid theory. Besides, it's worth a lot of money. It'll give me the lifestyle I deserve too," Wendy said.

"They won't let you keep it," Lane said. "They'll make you give it back."

"They have to find it all first. And as soon as I get out of here, I'm selling most of it to the highest bidder," Wendy said.

"Then how will you prove you're right? If you sell it to a private collector?" Lane was stalling for time. She needed to come up with a plan, fast.

"Oh, I'll keep some of it. A few pieces that prove my theory. It's really a win-win," Wendy said, and the smirk on her face made Lane want to smack it off.

Lane glanced up the street. They were running out of time. And what about Meg? Lane needed to find her. "Wendy, keep the fucking stuff—just get down."

"I will—" Wendy's words were cut off by the sound of gunfire.

"What the bloody hell is that?" Lane asked.

"Sounds like the cavalry has arrived," Wendy said. "Now we need to move."

Suddenly, the ground shook beneath the sound of a huge explosion. It knocked Wendy off the roof of the car and sent her bag flying, and the contents tumbled out and scattered across the road.

"No!" Wendy cried, barely acknowledging the explosion. So desperate to keep hold of the treasure, she frantically began collecting it back up.

Lane turned and reached out to Lois, who she had pushed behind her and out of the way of Wendy's gun. Lois immediately came into her arms. She picked the little girl up. "Wendy, leave that. We need to go."

Lane felt Lois's arms tighten around her neck and her legs circle her waist in the way all little kids know how to do.

"I can't. I can't—it's mine," Wendy said, stuffing the items back in the bag as quickly as she could.

"We need to get inside. That explosion, it could be Sigmarsson." Lane tried reasoning with her again.

"I don't care. And you're going to help me," Wendy said and pointed the gun at Lane.

"How did you manage to keep hold of that?" Lane asked.

"Never you mind. Put her down and start collecting up the rest."

"Wendy—"

"Now."

Lane had no choice. With a gun pointed at her, she'd have to do what Wendy wanted. But she'd bide her time, and she'd watch. And when Wendy let down her guard, Lane would have her.

Lane put Lois down and kissed the top of her head. "Keep close to me. This shouldn't take long."

"The more you procrastinate, Lane, the longer we risk more zombies turning up," Wendy said.

Lane nodded and began to pick up Wendy's treasure.

Chapter Fourteen

Meg had just ducked into an alley when, from a distance, she watched Wendy take a header off the car. She'd tried not to laugh, but she'd failed.

The zombies weren't so smart. They couldn't climb, and if you got out of their line of sight, they lost track of you pretty quickly. Meg guessed that was what happened when you had goo for a brain.

Her plan had been to head up to Bradford and double back to the Governor. It was risky, but they'd done the beach to death, and she knew there were more places to hide in and duck into up on Bradford.

Just as she'd been about to come out of her hiding place, another huge explosion had ripped through the town, almost throwing her to her knees. It was followed by a rapid burst of more gunfire. Meg could have wept with joy. That had to be the military. They were finally here. Surely she and Lane and Lois and Wendy could hang on for another few minutes until the rescuers got to them?

Meg poked her head out of the alley again. The scent of burning hung heavily in the air. She looked up the street to where the gunfire had come from, but all she could see was smoke and dust.

Then she saw it.

Saw him.

Ivar Sigmarsson.

He emerged from the smoke like some kind of movie monster. Except this wasn't a movie, and he was horribly, dangerously real. That was why the gunfire stopped, Meg thought. Those soldiers probably hadn't stood a chance. Meg couldn't think about how many had been lost to the zombies. Or the fact that they would become new zombies. They increased their numbers every time they bit someone.

How many soldiers had the military sent in? And when they realized those were gone, how many would they send after them?

Their only chance was to take Wendy's treasure and put it back. Sure, Sigmarsson might be so pissed he had no intention of stopping what he was doing, but they had to try. What else could they do? All it took was one bite. One bite and you turned from yourself into a mindless killing, eating machine.

They could send the whole of the United States military down here, but it wouldn't make a difference. And when the authorities realized that? When they understood that there was no beating this thing with all their fancy weapons? Well, you didn't need to be a genius to know they'd probably nuke the place. They'd probably blow it to kingdom come, and any healthy people who were left would be blown to kingdom come with the rest of the zombies.

Meg stepped back into the alley, realizing she'd been out in the open too long. Now what? She was trapped here in this fucking alley. She had to find a way to get back to the Governor. Convince Wendy to give up the treasure. Or take it from her. After what she'd done to Lois—dragging her out of the Pig—she didn't deserve their consideration.

Meg decided she had no choice but to go back the way she'd come. Hopefully she'd avoid Sigmarsson.

❖

Lane heard him before she saw him. She was stuffing the last few items into Wendy's bag. The volume of his screech made her drop the bag and cover her ears.

"Pick it up," Wendy shouted to be heard above him.

Lane looked up at her—or rather into the barrel of her gun—and had the urge to shove the thing down Wendy's throat. She probably could if she wanted. But there was the chance Wendy would get off a shot first and kill her dead. Lane weighed it up for a second.

"I wouldn't. I may not look like it, but I'm an excellent shot. You'll be dead before you get near me," Wendy said. "Now hurry, we don't have much time."

We've run out of time, Lane thought. She looked down the street, and there he was, Ivar Sigmarsson and all his minions, some of them dressed in military uniforms, which was depressing. Clearly the army's intervention hadn't worked. He screeched again, and a blue mist began to swirl around him.

Lane guessed he would probably do a victory lap after this. He'd just destroyed soldiers from one of the best militaries in the world, and he was now in sight of the treasure he wanted so badly. There was no way out of this.

Lane sighed. Looked like it was curtains for them. She turned to Lois. "Get under the car if you can, Lois, and stay there."

Lois, who was standing next to Wendy, shook her head. "I can't. I'm scared."

"I know you are. But it's the only way. Just shuffle under there," Lane said.

There was a chance Meg was still out there and safe. Even if Sigmarsson took her and Wendy, there was a possibility Meg would find Lois. Not much chance, mind you, but enough to give it a go. If Lane could distract him for a second.

"Give me the bag," Wendy said.

"I thought you wanted me to pick up the rest of the stuff?"

"No time. Give it to me," Wendy said and gestured with the gun.

"Fine." Lane made as if to hand it to her but, instead, swung it back and smashed it into Wendy's face. Wendy stumbled backwards, the contents went flying again, and Lane tried to grab the gun.

Wendy was stronger than Lane had given her credit for.

"Give me the goddamn gun. You're going to kill us all," Wendy shouted.

"We're already dead, you idiot," Lane said and punched Wendy in the side of the head.

The gun went off with a deafening crack. Someone screamed.

❖

Meg looked up at the sound of thumping blades. A helicopter. There wasn't enough light to see who it belonged to, but she guessed it was military. Could helicopters carry bombs? She didn't know. But it passed overhead and was gone, so she guessed she didn't have to worry about being blown to kingdom come just yet.

Meg had made it onto Bradford and figured the next right turn would take her onto the right street for the Governor. She'd been surprised to make it this far without running into any zombies. The thought worried her. Where were they all? She had a horrible feeling she might know.

She was moving slowly, ducking in and out of front yards

and behind cars just in case. It was slow progress, but the last thing she wanted was to run right into a zombie. She had Lane's hammer, but the thought of using it made her feel sick.

Meg was crouched behind a car when she heard the screech. She covered her ears. It was definitely coming from the bottom of the street. And it was probably Sigmarsson. He'd either met up with more soldiers or he'd found Lane and the others. Meg resisted the urge to run towards the sound. That wasn't going to help the situation.

But when she heard the single gunshot, she forgot about all that and bolted for the Governor. The only thought in her head was Lane and Lois.

❖

Lane rolled onto her back, trying to shift Wendy off. Wendy was a dead weight on top of her. Lane didn't know which, if either, of them was shot. It was hard to tell. She tried to look around for Lois but couldn't see her. Hopefully that meant she was under the car.

Lane heaved and lifted Wendy off her. Wendy groaned. There was no blood, so the shot must have gone wild. She'd been lucky, but so had Wendy.

Lane stumbled to her feet and looked up the street. Ivar Sigmarsson was still there with his horde. He locked eyes with Lane, and Lane shivered. She felt pressure in her brain like he was trying to dig in. She stepped backwards. And tripped.

Sigmarsson let out another almighty shriek. The ground shook beneath Lane, who was now flat on her arse. The horde moved forward as one, like a wave. Lane reached out blindly for something to use against them even though she knew it was pointless. She slid backwards on her bum, pushing with her heels. This was it. Curtains. She wondered where Wendy was but didn't dare take her eyes off the zombies marching slowly towards her.

Ouch, fuck! Lane shuffled back onto something sharp. She reached beneath her and felt cold hard metal. It wasn't the gun, thank God, or she might have blown her arse off. It was a knife. The one from Wendy's treasure.

Lane slid it out from beneath her and held it up. It was glowing. What the fuck? That wasn't right. Why was it glowing? And why was it so warm to the touch when it had been cold, seconds ago?

Suddenly, the world tilted on its axis and then went black.

❖

"Arn. Arn, wake up."

The first thing Lane was aware of was a soft rocking. Like being on a boat. The second thing was that whoever had just spoken to her had done it in a language that wasn't English, but she understood it anyway.

"I don't speak your language," she said. Except she did. She just had. How was that possible?

"Come on, Arn. Stop playing around. Eriksson wants to speak with you. You know he doesn't like to be kept waiting," the voice said again, and Lane opened her eyes.

She was on a ship—that much she knew. And then the word *knarr* came to her, and she knew that was the boat she was on. A cargo ship. She knew there were six men on board beside herself and that they'd damaged the front end of the boat. Lane knew they were less than a day from land. From Provincetown.

"I mean it, Arn. You should come now."

Lane sat up and rubbed her face with her hands. Her skin

was chapped and dry, and she was cold. She looked down at herself and saw she was covered in fur and skins, and what the bloody hell was going on? Not even her hands were her hands. They were large and male and had hair on the knuckles.

"Give me a moment," she said to the man—Bjorn was his name and she'd been friends with him since they were children. Except that wasn't right either. And she was speaking this strange language as if she had all her life. And weren't her thoughts now in this language too?

Lane stood, and where her right hand rested at her side she felt her knife, her langseax. She'd had that since she was a child, given to her by her father, and to him by his father before him.

Lane felt dizzy and like she was in a dream. Maybe she was. Or maybe she was dead. Ivar Sigmarsson had killed her, and she was in some fucked-up afterlife. Except that wasn't right. She'd picked up the Viking knife, and now she was here. Transported, maybe, to another place, another time?

That sounded completely insane, but then a bunch of zombies rampaging through a seaside town was also insane and that happened too.

Lane stood. "Let's go."

She followed Bjorn down the length of the boat, easily managing to stay upright despite the swaying. The boat was beautiful with a huge white sail and fewer oars than she imagined from the pictures she'd seen of Viking boats. It was wider than most Viking boats too and had a large amount of cargo in the middle. Because it was a knarr. A cargo ship for trading. Lane understood this, along with all the knowledge of the body she was now inhabiting. She was sure that if she needed to, she could navigate by the stars and wield the wicked-looking knife at her side with ease.

As she made her way along the boat, she bumped into

a man and instinctively pulled back from him. "Sorry," she mumbled.

"Watch where you're going," he replied.

"Sorry," she repeated.

The man was dressed in the same clothes as her, but they were much better quality. He was rich. Ivar Sigmarsson. Lane was simultaneously afraid of him and repulsed by him. He was cruel and dangerous, and the moment she looked into his eyes, she knew it was him. Ivar Sigmarsson. She'd been right.

Ivar Sigmarsson was Thorvold's cousin, and the only reason he was on this ship was as a favour. They were going across the Atlantic. All the way to North America—except the word was different in this language, and there wasn't a United States yet. There wasn't much of anything, as far as they knew. But they'd been sent off course during a storm, and the stern of the ship was damaged. Thorvold had ordered them to sail more southerly than they would have normally to avoid the storm.

"Arn, isn't it?" he asked.

"Yes, Sirl." Lane started to walk away, but he moved into her path.

"Perhaps you could do me a favour," he said, then carried on speaking as though she'd already agreed. "My cousin wants to dock up ahead instead of continuing on. I know he listens to you. Convince him to do otherwise. I'll make it worth your while."

Lane did her best to keep her dislike for the man off her face. "I serve Thorvold Eriksson, and any advice I give him will be in his interests."

Lane watched as his eyes widened and then narrowed again. They were sly eyes, full of cruelty, and Lane knew she had made an enemy.

"Very well," was all he said before he turned away, effectively dismissing her.

Lane could see land in the distance. They weren't far from it, maybe a few short hours.

The man at the end of the ship was a stranger to Lane, and yet somehow he wasn't. They'd sailed together countless times, and Lane was one of his favourites. He trusted her. She trusted him. Which was strange because they'd never actually met.

"Arn," he said and grinned at her. "You took your time. Too much to drink last night?"

"You should know—you gave it to me," she replied, and the words of this strange language rolled off her tongue without engaging her brain at all. It was as if she was a puppet.

"I did, that's true," he said. "I want your opinion. This land up ahead. Have you ever docked there before?"

Lane shook her head. "No, it's further south than I'd normally go, but the storm…"

"Yes, it knocked us off course. I'm trying to decide whether we dock there or take our chances and dock at our usual place."

Lane thought about it. Except she didn't really think about it because *Lane* had no idea. But the person she was right now, the body she was inhabiting, seemed to have a firm opinion. "We dock here. There's plenty of resources in this land. We can make the repairs and be on our way. Plus, we lost some provisions in the storm. We could go hunting while the men fix the ship."

Thorvold nodded. "That's what I think too."

"So what's stopping you, then?" Lane asked.

Thorvold nodded to where Sigmarsson sat in the middle of the knarr. "He wants to be on his way. He has furs and jewels and weapons to trade."

Lane shrugged. "But it's not his boat, is it?"

Thorvold laughed. "True, but it's his money that bought the boat. And the supplies on board."

"And he thinks that gives him authority over you?"

Thorvold's face changed then, full of thunder. "No one has authority over me. I'm the son of a king. His father may be rich and powerful, but he's a jarl and nothing more."

Lane nodded. "And we're taking a risk by continuing to sail with this damage. He must understand that."

Thorvold sighed, and the thunder passed out of him as quickly as it came. "He understands nothing of sailing and boats. He only understands money and possessions and power. My father hates him, you know."

Lane understood this was dangerous territory. It was one thing to take Thorvold's side out here on the ocean, but Ivar was his family, flesh and blood, and Lane knew getting involved in whatever dispute they had going was dangerous. "Well, he's staying put when we dock, so at least we won't have to take him back with us."

Thorvold nodded. "That's true. I think he's bad luck. The quicker he's off my boat, the better."

Lane understood that she was dismissed now, so she made her way back down to the bow of the boat. On her way past, Ivar Sigmarsson grabbed her arm. "What did he say? Are we going on?"

Lane pulled her arm free of his grasp. Her arm burned where he'd touched her, which was stupid because that shouldn't be possible. "No, we're docking. It's the right thing to do," she said.

Sigmarsson nodded, and Lane could see his sly brain working. "Very well. Did you tell him he should do that?"

"He already wanted to, and I agreed it was the best plan.

And it is. It's too dangerous to go on. What's a few more days to you, anyway?" Lane asked.

She was surprised when he grabbed her by the neck and pushed her against the mast.

"I'll lose my buyer and more money than you could ever hope to see in your miserable life, you little street rat," he said. With his face close to hers, Lane could smell his rancid breath. Given all the months spent on this boat, she knew hers wouldn't exactly be sweet, but there was something about this man that was rotten and fetid, and it was coming out of every pore.

Lane pushed him away from her, and he stumbled backwards before tripping and landing on his arse. Not good. Not good at all. The men around her began to laugh.

Lane stepped forward and offered her hand to help him to his feet. She hadn't intended to knock him to the floor. She might lose her life for this. A person didn't push over the nephew of a king.

Sigmarsson pushed her hand away and got quickly to his feet. He was agile. "Get away from me," he said. "You'll pay for this, street rat."

Lane felt fear bubble up inside her. She didn't want to die. Maybe Thorvold would take pity on her and leave her behind when they docked. That could be her punishment.

"What's going on here?" Thorvold asked. He must have heard the commotion.

"This insubordinate little shit pushed me down," Sigmarsson said.

Thorvold looked at her. "Is that true?"

"I pushed him away from me when he grabbed me. But yes, I did push him down," she said.

"Punish him. Throw him overboard," Sigmarsson said.

Lane's stomach dropped. She'd seen it done before, and it wasn't a nice way to go.

"I think that's a bit harsh," Thorvold said. "Sounds like it was an accident. And you grabbed him first."

"I don't believe this. I don't. You're taking his side, cousin?" Sigmarsson said.

"I'm not taking anyone's side."

"He has insulted you and the King by his actions, but you stand there and tell me you won't punish him. I never knew you were such a weak man," Sigmarsson said.

"I'm not weak—"

Before Thorvold could finish, Sigmarsson drew his seax and lunged at Lane. She stepped back and turned to the side to dodge him. He meant to kill her—that much was clear.

"Ivar," Thorvold said.

"If you won't defend our family's honour, then I will." Sigmarsson lunged at her again, and when Lane feinted left, he read it and slashed at her, catching her side and opening a wound that began to gush blood.

Lane hissed at the pain. What should she do now? Fight him and risk killing him? That would certainly mean her death. Thorvold couldn't allow her to live after that. Or she could keep dodging him, but he was fast and would likely end up killing her.

Sigmarsson came at her again, and she jumped out of the way, narrowly avoiding his blade. A crowd had gathered to watch, and out of the corner of her eye, Lane saw Thorvold had stepped back. Which meant he was not going to interfere.

"I meant you no disrespect," she said to Sigmarsson.

Sigmarsson slashed at her again and tore a hole in her shirt. "Fight me like a man," he said. "Stop dodging."

Lane moved behind the mast. It would be difficult for him

to slash at her that way. She had to think of a way to disarm him without hurting him. It was the only way to keep her life.

"I don't want to fight you, Sirl," she said and moved to the left when he tried to come around the mast.

"You should have thought about that, shouldn't you," he said.

Lane stepped back again, avoiding the ropes curled on the deck. Maybe she could wear him out. Keep him talking and make him see sense.

He stalked her, and she realized she would have no option but to fight him if she wanted to live.

Lane—or Arn?—drew her blade. She tried to reason with him one last time. "Please, Sirl. Let's not do this. It was an accident."

"Shut your mouth and fight me. After I kill you, I'll find your family and kill them too. I'll make your wife my slave, and I'll cut your children's throats in front of her," Sigmarsson said.

Lane came at him then. Her wife and children hadn't been threatened—they were Arn's—but she knew all the same that he wasn't making an idle threat. Through Arn, Lane knew everything about Sigmarsson that she needed to know. He was rotten to the core. He would do all the things he said he would. And for what? An accident.

Lane thrust the knife forward, and he sidestepped, then parried by lunging at her again. He missed.

They circled each other, each looking for some weakness in the other. Lane knew she was a better fighter, but he was sneaky and quick. She made as if to lunge again, and when he sidestepped left, she went with him. Lane buried the knife in his chest.

Sigmarsson dropped to his knees clutching the knife in

his chest. He looked up at her in disbelief. "You stabbed me. I'll get you for this." Then he fell forward, flat onto his face, and was still.

When Sigmarsson didn't move, one of the other men approached him and knelt down. He turned him by his shoulder, and Lane heard the man's sharp intake of breath.

"Oh, dear. Arn, you killed him."

Lane felt sick. She couldn't care less about Sigmarsson, but this surely meant she'd have to die. She'd killed the relative of a king. She'd had no choice but that wouldn't matter.

"Let me see," Thorvold said.

He flipped Sigmarsson onto his back with his foot. "You're right. He's definitely dead."

Thorvold bent down and pulled the knife out of his chest. He wiped the blade on Sigmarsson's shoulder and passed it to Lane. "Here. It's a good knife. Too good to stay in that idiot. But when we bury him, you must leave it there with him."

Lane took it, stunned. "But what about—"

"Let's say no more about it," Thorvold said. And then, to the other men on the ship, "Did you hear that? We'll say no more about it."

The other men nodded and started to wander off back to their chores.

"When we dock, we'll bury him with all his shit," Thorvold said. "Don't want the fucker coming back as a draugr, do we?"

"What do you mean, a draugr?" Lane asked. Through Arn, she already knew most of it, but she wanted it said out loud.

"Come on now, Arn. You know what a draugr is," Thorvold said. "There's no one in the world as vicious as Ivar. If anyone's going to come back from the dead, it's him. Best to make sure that doesn't happen. We'll bury him upside down too, so he can't find his way back out of the grave."

"And with all his possessions because he's greedy enough to come looking for them," Lane added.

"And the knife that killed him. It's a shame to lose such a good one, but if he does come back, he won't want to see that again," Thorvold said.

"And whoever finds it can use it to kill him again," Lane said.

"Yes. Are you all right?" Thorvold asked.

"I think so. I think I am now," she replied.

Thorvold squeezed her shoulders. "There was nothing to be done. These men won't talk. And I won't be throwing you overboard or anything silly like that."

They docked in Provincetown several hours later. Lane helped the other men carry Sigmarsson off the boat. They walked for a long time with his dead weight on their shoulders before Thorvold was satisfied with the burial site.

"We'll leave him here. It's far enough inland. Make sure you bury him deep," Thorvold said.

Lane helped dig the grave. They went down eight feet before Thorvold was happy. They placed him head first with his feet to the sky. Lane shovelled earth over him to cover him completely before they put the treasure box in.

Thorvold had ordered meats and beer and clothing to go in with him. They also put in Sigmarsson's jewellery—of which he had a lot—and her much loved knife.

"There," Thorvold said when the grave was completely filled in. "He'll cause no more trouble. Let's just hope no one ever digs him up. They'll be in for a nasty surprise if that bugger ever comes back."

You have no idea, Lane thought but kept quiet. He would come back, she knew. And he'd wreak havoc. And Wendy would know all about it and not say a word.

CHAPTER FIFTEEN

Lane stumbled and cried out as the world came back into focus. What the bloody hell had that all been about?

She looked down at her hand and saw she was still holding the knife. It was glowing bright and felt hot in her hand.

She looked up and saw the zombies had stopped in their tracks. Their low groans had a hint of confusion to them, and several looked back at Sigmarsson. They weren't sure what to do, Lane realized. Something about this knife.

Lane held the knife up above her head like she was some cut-price King Arthur and was astonished to see the zombies shrink back.

"Come on," she shouted, feeling more confident than she probably should. "Come on then if you want some."

The zombies started moving backwards. The groans became louder, and Lane swore they sounded scared. This knife was a talisman, something to do with that weird hallucination she'd just had. It was mad, but she didn't care if it worked.

Sigmarsson wasn't looking too great either. He'd stepped back several paces. Something about this knife had unnerved him, and Lane had a feeling she knew what it was. He'd been killed by this knife all those years ago, and somehow it had power. Maybe the power to kill him all over again.

Lane walked forward a few paces with the knife still held above her. "Don't like it, do you?" she cried. "Not nice when the shoe's on the other foot, is it?"

Again, they shrunk away, and even better, so did Sigmarsson.

Inside Lane, something snapped. All the fear and the sadness and the desperation she'd been feeling over the last twenty-four hours came to a head.

Lane charged them. Screaming at the top of her lungs, she slashed at one zombie and almost took his head clean off. She spun and pushed the blade through the throat of another. Unlike with the hammer, which you had to aim at their heads, the knife seemed to kill them dead wherever she got them.

Lane slashed and hacked her way through a sea of zombies, and not one of them bit her or came at her. Like the Red Sea, they parted. The knife terrified them. Just like they'd terrified her. The knife cut through them like butter and killed them on the spot, just like they'd killed Teensy.

But the main target, the one she was working her way towards, the architect of all this destruction and death, would bear the brunt of her rage. All of this started and finished with him. Lane would put him down, and she didn't care what happened to her. As long as he was dead. She'd managed it before—albeit accidentally—and she'd do it again.

But when she got through the crowds of zombies, he'd gone. Lane looked around. He'd disappeared. It was impossible. He was nearly seven feet tall and not exactly easy to miss. Where the hell did he go?

The zombies were also melting away, shuffling off down alleys and side streets. Lane stood in the middle of the road and wasn't sure what to do next. He was gone. She had to find him and kill him. But how? Where would he go? Where *did* he go?

And then she realized. Where he'd been buried. Lane racked her brain for that newspaper article she'd read on the plane a million years ago. Where had those workmen found the treasure?

Winthrop Street. Lane vaguely remembered it from the other day, but Meg would know exactly where that was. If she was still alive. Please God, she was still alive. She had to be.

Lane turned and started to walk back to the Governor. Then she saw her. Meg. Lane was equal parts elated and equal parts sick to her stomach. She was with Wendy. And Wendy had a gun to her head.

❖

Meg cursed herself. How could she have been so stupid? When she heard the gunshot, she'd flown down the street. What she saw had stopped her dead in her tracks.

Lane was standing in the middle of Commercial with some kind of knife in her hand, and it was on fire. It burned so bright, Meg had to shield her eyes. At first she'd been worried Lane would get hurt, but when she looked again, she saw that Lane wasn't bothered by it at all.

How was that possible?

Meg didn't have time to think about that because with a war cry Lane was charging into the zombies, and they were moving *away* from her. The knife scared them. And it scared Sigmarsson too. Meg let out a whoop.

"Impressive, isn't she?" Wendy said from behind her.

Meg turned. Straight into the barrel of a gun. "What the fuck, Wendy? Where is everybody getting fucking guns from in fucking Massachusetts?"

"You know, I found this in my father's stuff when he died. I almost threw it in the ocean because I was so worried about having an unlicensed firearm. Glad I kept it now." Wendy motioned with the gun. "Get back here with me and Lois. We're going to wait this thing out."

And now Meg was standing in front of a car. Wendy had moved the gun so that it was now pressed into the small of her back. Wendy was using her in a hostage negotiation.

"You can have your little girlfriend. Just give me the knife," Wendy said to Lane. She pushed the bag over with her foot. "Put it in there."

Meg locked eyes with Lane and shook her head. There was no way Lane should exchange her for the knife. That knife was going to save Lane and Lois.

"Stay out of it, Meg," Wendy said and pushed the gun more firmly into Meg's back.

"I will not stay out of it. Wendy, think about it. We could kill Sigmarsson with that knife. Take the rest of the treasure if you want it, but leave Lane the knife."

"Meg has a point. Why—" Lane was cut off.

"Shut up, shut up, shut up. Both of you, shut up. Lane, you've got five seconds to make up your mind. Either give me the knife, or I shoot your little girlfriend," Wendy said.

Meg looked at Lane again and tried to convey how much she didn't want Lane to hand it over.

"How do I know you won't shoot her anyway?" Lane asked.

Wendy shrugged. "I guess you don't. You'll have to do it on trust."

"Trust? You've proven throughout this whole thing that the last thing you are is trustworthy, Wendy."

"You have a point. Look, I need the knife to get out of here with the treasure. It obviously keeps those things away. I also don't want to use any more bullets than I need to," Wendy said. "I'd rather save them for the zombies."

It made sense, Meg thought. "And what will you do when you get to Boston or wherever it is you're going? You don't think anyone's going to ask where you got that treasure from? You don't think they'll make you hand it in?"

"I thought about that. I've met a few collectors in my time, and they know other collectors. I don't imagine I'll have much trouble selling it," Wendy said.

"But I thought the whole reason you took it was because you believe it belongs in Provincetown?" Lane said.

"It does. But look around, not much of Provincetown left. I can't imagine it'll be long before the military bomb this place off the map. I've worked my whole life in this town. I know people laughed at me. *Oh look, it's Wendy and her stupid little library exhibitions again.* Well, now they're dead—or zombies—so who's laughing? I deserve to retire in style. And this stuff is worth a lot of money."

"You never cared about whether it stayed here or not," Meg said.

"Yes, I did. But plans change. Now, we've talked long enough. Put the knife in the bag, Lane, or I will shoot Meg. You know I will."

Meg watched as Lane looked down at the knife in her hand, then looked at Meg. Meg shook her head again.

"I'm sorry, Meg, but it was never a choice," Lane said. She bent down and put the knife in the bag.

"Good, now kick the bag over here carefully. Don't break anything."

Lane did as she was told. She pushed the bag with her foot. "Here, take it. I hope it brings you nothing but misery."

"Pick up the bag, Meg," Wendy said and nudged Meg in the back.

"Me? You said you'd let me go if she gave it to you," Meg said.

"And I will. In a minute. I kind of have my hands full right now. Pick up the bag," Wendy said.

Meg bent down and picked up the bag. It was heavy and it clanged.

"Now, put the straps over your shoulders, Meg—and no funny business. Lane, I want you to call Lois out from under that car. We're going for a little walk."

No," Lane said. Then she shouted, "Lois, you stay under there. Don't come out."

Meg felt a sharp pain in her lower back. At first, she thought maybe Wendy shot her, but the gun hadn't gone off. "Jesus, stop. Ow," Meg said.

"Pull another trick like that, and I'll pull the trigger. Right on her spine," Wendy said to Lane.

That was when Meg realized Wendy was truly serious. It wasn't exactly that she'd doubted her before, but Wendy was…Wendy. She came into the bar every night for a glass of wine, and they made small talk. Everyone knew Wendy—she'd been in the town her whole life. Meg thought she was nice if a little dull. It just went to show you never really knew anyone until the shit hit the fan. That was when people's true colours came out.

"Fine, fine. Just don't hurt her," Lane said.

"Lois?" Wendy called out. "Come on out, or I'm going to hurt one of your little friends again. You hear me, honey?"

Meg turned her head slightly to watch Lois slide out from under the car. The poor kid looked terrified. "It's okay," Meg said, realizing how much of a lie that was.

"Please don't hurt them," Lois said.

"As long as they do what they're told—as long as you *all* do what you're told—I won't have to," Wendy replied. "Now the gang's all here."

Meg rolled her eyes. She was really getting to hate Wendy Moon. "What's your plan now?"

"We're going for a little stroll down to Whalers Wharf," Wendy said.

"What? Why?" Lane asked, hoping to stall for time but picking her own bag up anyway.

"You'll see. Now move. Lane in front, Lois behind her, and Meg in front of me. If anyone so much as twitches, I'm going to shoot Meg," Wendy said.

The four of them made their way down a deserted Commercial Street.

❖

"Why are we at Whalers Wharf?"

Lane heard the confusion in Meg's voice. She daren't turn around to look at Meg, even though she'd been dying to do just that during the walk down here.

Lois was holding on to the back of Lane's jeans, and every now and then Lane would risk reaching back to briefly squeeze Lois's hand. The little girl must be absolutely terrified.

Lane didn't want to look back at Meg, though, and do anything to make Wendy hurt her. It seemed Wendy was on a knife-edge. Lane hadn't known her before all this kicked off, but she doubted she had been this unstable before. Something about the treasure, maybe.

Lane thought back to the hallucination she'd had earlier. Ivar Sigmarsson. He was rotten through and through, and maybe something of him had seeped into the treasure. Or maybe she was making excuses for Wendy. Perhaps Wendy was actually a selfish and cruel person.

Lane heard Meg again ask why they were at Whalers

Wharf. They'd walked right past MacMillan Pier, where she would presumably take Teensy's boat back to the mainland.

"Because it's somewhere safe I can put you," Wendy said.

"What do you mean?" Lane asked.

"Keep moving. Go on, all the way through," Wendy said, ignoring the question.

They walked past the shops which flanked them on either side. Lane had been here before, for her tarot reading. Back when the biggest thing on her mind was getting Meg back. She shook her head. Funny how things turned out. She adjusted the bag on her shoulder. Just past the last shop on the right was a door with *Bathroom* written on it.

"Stop," Wendy said, and they all came to a halt. "Okay, Lane and Lois, go in there."

"Here?" Lane looked into a dingy public toilet. "You want us to go in there?"

"Yes. In there. Don't test me," Wendy said.

"But it's dark in there. And it smells funny," Lois said.

"I don't care. Move," Wendy said, and Lane heard Meg gasp.

Lane didn't need to look around to know that Wendy had probably jabbed her with the gun. "Okay, okay. Just leave her alone."

Lane reached behind her and took Lois's hand. "We have to be really brave now, Lois," she said. "I won't let anything hurt you in here."

"Okay, Lane," Lois said.

Lane led Lois into the toilet and hoped that was true.

"Back against the far wall. Both of you," Wendy called. Lane guided Lois backwards until her back touched the wall. She tried not to think about what might be on the tiles.

"Good," Wendy said. "Now you, Meg. And don't make

any sudden moves. You know I'm a good shot, and I'll drop you before you get anywhere near me."

Lane knew it was the truth and prayed Meg wouldn't do anything stupid. She watched as Meg came towards her. She put her bag down on the grubby floor and tried not to think about the last time it had been cleaned.

"Meg, up against the wall too. That's right, well done. Take the bag off slowly," Wendy said. "Put it on the ground."

Now all three of them were standing against the toilet wall. Lane waited to see what Wendy would do. It didn't escape her notice that this was a good position for a firing-squad style execution. If it came to it, she'd shield Lois with her own body. Meg would understand. Meg would probably do the same.

Lane had never felt so hopeless or unsure in her life. Should she charge Wendy? It was true Wendy could drop her easily, but Lane wasn't small. She reckoned she could tackle Wendy to the ground even with a bullet hole in her.

Lane stepped forward. "Wendy, you don't have to do this."

"Get back against that wall. I mean it. I will shoot you," Wendy said and raised the gun.

Lane swallowed and stood her ground. "We won't give you any trouble—just let us come with you."

"You should have thought of that before you decided to take my treasure. I would have let you come with me, you know."

Lane moved over in an effort to shield Meg. "I'm sorry."

"Too late, and I swear to God if you don't move back against that wall, Lane…"

Lane held up her hands in surrender. "Okay, okay." She moved back and stood against the wall.

"Now kick that bag over. Slide it along the floor," Wendy said to Meg.

Lane watched as Meg shoved the bag with her foot.

In one smooth movement, Wendy picked up the bag and quickly swing the door shut, and Lane heard the lock turn from the outside.

Wendy's muffled voice came from the other side. "This is the safest place for you. If the military don't blow Provincetown to smithereens, they'll find you and let you out. I left the key in the door. At least the zombies can't get to you in here, and I don't think they can turn keys."

Lane jumped when Meg launched herself at the door with a howl of fury. "You bitch, Wendy. You goddamn bitch. How could you do this to us? To a small child?"

But Wendy didn't answer. Lane guessed she was gone, on her way to the pier and then to Boston. Lane almost smiled.

"Hey, Meg, did you do it?" she asked.

"I did. Now all we have to do is figure a way out of here," Meg said.

Lane looked around the bathroom. Nothing was immediately obvious. The door looked too strong to break down, but she'd give it a go anyway.

Lane was so deep in her own thoughts, she was surprised when Lois tugged on her arm.

"What's that, sweetheart?" Lane asked.

"Up there. Look." Lois pointed to the ceiling.

Lane looked up. And smiled.

Chapter Sixteen

Wendy moved with confidence. The bag was secured on her shoulders, and she would not hesitate to use the knife inside it if the need arose. The bag was lighter than before, but she guessed some of treasure had been lost outside the Governor. Hopefully not *too* much. She wanted as much money as she could get from it when she sold it. As soon as she was safely on the boat, she'd go through it and do an inventory.

She half wanted to bump into Sigmarsson, as Lane called him. If only she'd known sooner about the knife's power, she could have saved Teensy. That would be her one regret, she thought. But it wasn't meant to be. She felt kind of bad about Meg and the little girl, but she told herself she'd left them somewhere safe. Another person might just have shot them all or left them to die out on the street.

Wendy had gone out of her way to take them somewhere safe. It was true that the military might nuke them, but that wasn't her fault. She'd done all she could for them.

After years in this town surrounded by people who had no appreciation for her work, she was finally getting out. In a way, Wendy felt like maybe that treasure had been meant for her all along. It seemed strange that of all things to finally get her the life she deserved, it was treasure from a long-dead Viking. A people she'd been studying and writing about for years. She wrote her first academic paper on Thorvold Eriksson and the theory that he'd come to Provincetown. Now not only did she have proof, but she had the treasure right here in her bag. Treasure that was going to make her a very rich woman indeed.

When she'd first set eyes on the jewellery, she'd known immediately it was worth a lot. Not just for the value of the gold and silver but because it was a rare find. Some of the artifacts she knew would be sought after by museums and private collectors alike. There were some stunning examples and all so well preserved.

Wendy made her way across the parking lot at MacMillan Pier. She barely glanced up and was so lost in her own thoughts, she almost didn't notice the zombies that had begun to gather behind her.

Wendy walked onto the pier and found Teensy's boat slip. Tied up, just like she said it would be, was *Dawn's Crack*. It was small but, Wendy knew, perfectly maintained. She took the bag of treasure off and put it on the ground. She hadn't had a chance to properly look at it before, but she would now.

Before she could open the bag, Wendy heard a moan. Then another one. She looked up.

Wendy gasped. There were maybe thirty zombies, though Ivar Sigmarsson wasn't among them. They had totally blocked off her exit back along the pier. Not that it mattered.

She leaned down slowly and started to untie the boat, never taking her eyes off them. They moved forward slowly, cautiously, as if they remembered their last encounter with Wendy and her group. Wendy stopped fiddling with the ropes. They were loose, but she didn't want the boat floating off before she had a chance to get in it.

Wendy reached into the bag at her feet and felt around for

the knife. Something didn't feel right, though. Was that a fork? What the hell?

Ignoring the zombies coming towards her, Wendy pulled open the bag and looked inside.

Cutlery. Knives and forks and spoons and even a spatula. She screamed in frustration. Those cheating, lying bastards. They'd stolen from her. Taken it all. They must have switched the bags when she wasn't looking.

At least she still had the gun. She'd find a way through this mob and get back to Whalers Wharf. She'd kill them all. Bullet to the chest for each of them. God damn them!

The zombies kept on coming for her.

As the zombies started to advance, Wendy pulled the gun from her waistband and aimed it at them.

She had maybe five shots. It should be enough to hit a few and save some bullets for the others and give her time to get on the boat. She figured she could sail down to Whalers Wharf and deal with them.

Wendy fired a shot at the zombie closest to her. Its head exploded yellow goo, and she felt a measure of satisfaction. But they were gaining on her all the time.

Wendy quickly turned and worked on the ropes tethering the boat to the dock. Damn, Teensy had tied them tight. Wendy pushed her fingers through a knot and tried to prise it loose, but her hands were greasy with sweat and shaking.

She looked up just in time to see the first zombie reach her. It wasn't fair. It wasn't supposed to be this way. She was supposed to get away on the boat, all the way to Boston. Wendy was meant to have a good life—she'd led a good life up until now. This just wasn't fair.

The first zombie bit into Wendy's arm, the arm with the gun, and she howled in pain. Her arm was on fire, and she watched as the blood splashed onto her shoes and soaked into the ground.

Wendy stumbled backward, and her arm lit up with pain again, as flesh was torn from it. Part of her arm hung out of the zombie's mouth, and Wendy felt sick.

The next zombie that came was tall, and it bent its head and bit into her neck. Wendy beat at it with her fists, but it just kept on biting and tearing. The pain set off bright white lights behind Wendy's eyes, and she prayed she would pass out before they bit her again.

She fell, half in and half out the boat. Something attached itself to her leg, and she heard and felt a crunch. Thankfully, she didn't feel the pain because she passed out before she was eaten alive.

❖

Meg wrapped her legs around Lane's waist and pushed with her arms. The loose ceiling tile moved easily enough.

"Can you see how much room is up there?" Lane asked.

"Give me a second, Lane," Meg said.

Lois had been the one to spot the loose tile. She might just have saved all their lives. If there was enough room to crawl through.

Above the tile were a whole lot of pipes and tubes. Also the beams they sat on didn't look strong enough to hold a full-grown woman.

"Okay, let me down," Meg said.

She enjoyed the contact with Lane's body as she slid down the length of her to the ground. Probably not the best time to be thinking about *that*.

"Well? Is it a goer?" Lane asked full of hope.

Meg felt bad. "No, I don't think so. The pipes are too

low to the tiles, and I don't think the beams would hold our weight."

Meg put down the seat on the questionably unsanitary toilet and sat down. At this point, she had more to worry about than a few germs.

"I might fit," Lois said.

"No, honey. It's too dangerous," Meg said.

"I don't know that we have a choice, Meg," Lane said.

"It's not far to the other side," Lois said. "I can jump down just like I did in my apartment when you found me." She put her hand on Meg's knee. "Don't worry, I can do it."

"What if Wendy lied about the key?" Meg asked. "What if she didn't leave it in the door?"

Lane sighed and rubbed her eyes. "Meg, we've tried kicking the door in and it won't budge. I think this is our only option. If there's no key, then..."

"Then Lois is stuck on the other side by herself," Meg finished.

"Yeah. Yeah, you're right. Lois, it's not going to work," Lane said.

"Please let me try. If there's no key, I'll get a chair and boost myself back up. I swear," Lois said and crossed her chest with her hand.

Meg almost smiled. Lois was so young. The idea of her being trapped on the other side without them made Meg feel ill. But really, what was the alterative? Sit in here and wait for the military to blow them up or let them out? And what if it wasn't the military that came? What if it was Sigmarsson?

"Okay, fine. But promise me if there's no key, you'll get a chair from one of the stores and come right back," Meg said.

"I swear it," Lois said.

"Okay then," Meg replied, feeling all kinds of guilty.

"Come on, sweetheart," Lane said. "I'll boost you up."

Meg watched as Lane easily lifted the little girl up into the cavity above the ceiling tile. Lois wriggled into the space and then disappeared.

"Lois," Lane called, "before you jump down, look to make sure there's no zombies out there."

"Okay," came Lois's muffled reply.

Meg went to the bathroom door, and the two of them pressed their ears to it. Meg could hear a thump and hoped it was Lois jumping down.

"You okay, Lois? Didn't hurt yourself?" Meg called out.

"No, ma'am. I'm fine," Lois replied.

In a few moments, they heard the lock scrape and click, and then the handle went down, and Lois was pushing open the door.

When she saw her, Lane laughed, whooped, and picked Lois up. She swung her around and kissed the top of her head. "Our hero."

Meg ruffled her hair. "Well done, honey."

Lois smiled and laughed. "See? I told you I could do it. My mom says I'm like a monkey."

"And you are. You definitely are." Lane swung her around one more time, then put her back on the ground.

"Okay," Meg said. "Let's get out of here."

❖

Lane tried not to think about Wendy. It was true Wendy had left them to their fate and probably would have killed them if it'd come to it, but Lane felt bad nonetheless. They'd written Wendy's death warrant.

"You need to stop feeling guilty, Lane," Meg said.

"I know. But I can't help it," Lane replied.

"She left us for dead. She didn't exactly leave us much choice."

"True, but we aren't like her. I'm allowed to feel bad about what we did," Lane said.

Meg didn't reply.

Commercial Street was quiet. Lane was relieved and worried at the same time. Earlier, the zombies had disappeared as if by magic. It was true she had the knife, but there was no guarantee it would work a second time.

They made their way carefully along the street, stopping every so often to listen out for the telltale groan of an approaching zombie.

Soon they were back at the Squealing Pig. The same place they always ended up. It didn't matter where they got to, the Pig always seemed to be the destination.

Lane hammered the door shut behind them. They didn't have much time and they had a lot to plan.

"Drink?" Meg called from the bar.

"Not for me. I want a clear head," Lane replied.

"Will it bother you if I have one?" Meg asked.

"Not at all. I think the next part is mostly on me anyway," Lane said.

Meg started to protest, and then closed her mouth. She'd been there back at the Governor. She'd seen what had happened with the knife. For whatever reason, Lane was the one who needed to kill Ivar Sigmarsson with the langseax.

"I need to tell you something," Lane said. "Both of you."

Lois was only small but she'd been the one to get them out of the toilet, and she was just as much a part of this as any of them.

"Sounds serious," Meg said. "You sure you don't want a drink?"

Lane nodded. "I'm sure. It's about what happened with the knife."

"When it lit up and scared the shit out of Sigmarsson?" Meg said.

"Yeah, exactly. Right before it did that, I went... somewhere."

"Uh-uh. I saw you standing there the whole time," Lois said.

"I mean, in my mind," Lane said.

Meg joined them at the table and took a sip of wine. "Sounds interesting, do tell."

When Lane finished telling them the story of her encounter on the knarr, she felt better. It was a weird story, and she felt lighter for sharing it.

"Well," Meg said and took a big gulp of wine, "if I hadn't already seen what I've seen today, I'd say you were crazy and probably call the cops."

"But you believe me?" Lane asked, and it was desperately important that Meg did.

"Shit, why not? If I can believe in zombies and giants shooting blue flames out of their mouths, why not believe that you went back in time and met this guy before he became a zombie?"

"I'm not lying," Lane said.

Meg reached across the table and squeezed her hand. "I know you're not. But it's just so crazy."

"You have to kill him, Lane," Lois said. "You're like the hero in my book."

"What book?" Lane asked.

"My book about a boy who kills a dragon with a special sword. But the sword is only special for him. You're the hero, Lane."

"From the mouths of babes," Meg said and clinked cheers with Lane before knocking back the rest of the wine.

Lane didn't want to be the hero. She wanted to be back in her penthouse flat on the River Thames drinking expensive wine and talking shit with her stupid friends.

She did not want to be the hero of this story.

She did not want to slay the dragon.

But if not her, then who? Sure, she could do a Wendy and hightail it off in the boat. Forget this had ever happened and leave others to sort the mess out. She could do that, but she'd never be able to look Meg in the eye. All her life, she'd gone along without making any fuss, doing what she was told and living a life on the surface. This was her chance to show what she was really made of. To be Lois's storybook hero.

She knew there was a good chance she would die—that they would all die—but what other choice did she have?

Lane finally understood she was brave. Where other people gave up and gave in, she persevered. And she had to try. For Meg and for Lois and for the countless other people who had died or who would die because of Ivar Sigmarsson and Wendy Moon.

Lane was ready.

Chapter Seventeen

Meg didn't like the plan at all. She thought it was the worst plan she'd ever heard. She wanted more wine, but she didn't want to get drunk.

The plan wasn't a bad plan at all. In fact, it was probably the only plan. What she didn't like about it was that it involved Lane going up against Ivar Sigmarsson by herself. Meg didn't have to be a bookie to know the odds weren't good. They were still sitting at the table in the Pig, but not for much longer.

"I hate the plan," Meg said again for the twentieth time.

"I know you do, but it's the only way it'll work," Lane said.

"Not true. You could take me with you. We could wait for the military," Meg said.

"Because that worked out so well last time? Look, I'm sure they'll be back, but I'm betting it's from the sky. With lots of bombs. This way, you and Lois will be safe."

"And what about you?" Meg asked.

"I reckon it's fifty-fifty," Lane said.

Meg punched her lightly on the arm. "You're supposed to say you'll be fine. That's what the hero in the movie always tells the girl."

"Are you the girl, then? I always thought they were pretty

passive. I think you're better cast as the other hero," Lane said and grinned.

"So smooth," Meg said and rolled her eyes. "Come on, let's get this over with."

The three of them, Meg, Lane, and Lois, left the Squealing Pig for the last time. This was it. They'd made their plan, and it would work. It had to work because the alternative was too much to bear.

Meg had realized how much Lane meant to her and what a fool she'd been to throw it all away. Or maybe she was being too hard on herself. Lane seemed different. Meg guessed it was the situation. This crisis had brought out the worst in Wendy, but it had shown Meg who Lane really was. And, Meg suspected, facing this nightmare had probably shown Lane her true self too. Lane had never struck Meg as being all that confident despite her bluster. But maybe Provincetown had shown her just how brave and capable she really was.

And if Lane's true colours had finally come out, had Meg's? She wasn't unlike Wendy in a lot of ways. Obsessed with an idea, with work. Wendy's had been Vikings, and Meg's was her bar. Both of them were prepared to make huge sacrifices to get what they wanted. The only difference was Wendy was willing to sacrifice people for her dream.

Meg had been sacrificing herself. For years.

It was time for that to stop. And for her life to start with Lane. If Lane would have her. And if they made it out of this alive.

"We're here," Lane said quietly.

Meg was startled to realize they'd walked all the way to MacMillan Pier. "The boat should be up ahead unless Wendy got away."

They walked a little further. Meg smelled it before she

saw it. Blood mixed with salt. She put her hand on Lois's shoulder. "Wait here just a minute, honey."

Meg looked at Lane, and by unspoken agreement they walked further down the pier. Meg heard Lane suck in a breath when they saw it.

"You think that was Wendy?" Lane asked.

"Seems like kind of a coincidence if it's not. Look, the bag is in Teensy's boat." Meg pointed to the bag they'd switched back in the bathroom.

Lane nodded. "Looks like they got her pretty bad."

"But she got up." Meg pointed to the bloody footprints that went a few feet down the pier before they disappeared.

"Where do you think she went?" Lane asked.

Meg shrugged. "Into the water? Maybe she was injured but managed to get away. I know I'd go into the water."

"Either way, she's one of them now," Lane said.

Meg nodded. Lane started to say something again when a huge bang drowned her out. It was followed by rapid gunfire and more bangs. The steady thump of rotor blades started up overhead.

"Get Lois," Lane said, but Meg didn't need to be told and was already running back up the pier.

❖

Lane zipped up Lois's life jacket. "I'll see you in a little while, okay?"

Lois nodded. "You're the hero, remember? So you can't die."

"Yeah, I remember," Lane said and stroked a hand over Lois's head. She stood up and turned to face Meg. "I'll see you then," she said, suddenly feeling awkward.

"This doesn't seem right. I should be going with you," Meg said and brushed some nonexistent lint from Lane's shoulder.

"Someone needs to stay with Lois. If anything happens to me—"

"Don't say that."

"But I—"

"Don't say it, Lane."

And then Meg kissed her. It was a hard kiss, a claiming kiss that said she belonged to Meg. Lane shut her eyes and forced herself to feel every moment of it.

Meg's hands drifted down and squeezed her arse. Lane smiled into the kiss.

"This always was my favourite part of you," Meg said against her lips. And then, "What's this?"

Lane didn't know what she was talking about. Meg's hand pulled something out of her back pocket, and then Meg stepped back, examining the item—a card of some kind.

"Lane, what is this?" Meg asked again. She looked scared and confused.

"I don't—" Lane started to say. Meg turned the card around.

What the actual fuck? Lane snatched the card out of her hand. It was the tarot card she'd gotten what seemed like a lifetime ago.

The card depicted a woman in shining gold armour. She held a sword in her hand and looked like she was bringing it down on a grey figure below her.

"Lane," Meg said, "it's you."

And Meg was right. The woman on the card *was* her, but how could that be? What had the tarot reader said to her as she'd stuffed it into her hand? *You might need this.*

Lane didn't have time to go into it with Meg. If the cacophony up on Commercial was anything to go by, she was quickly running out of time. She put the card back in the back pocket of her jeans. "I'll explain later. I have to go."

Meg nodded. "You have the map I drew?"

"Yes." Lane nodded. She'd memorized that map back at the Pig. It was too important not to.

"And you have the treasure?" Meg asked.

"Yes, in the bag," Lane said.

"Okay, then. Good luck. And you'd better come back to me, Lane Boyd, or I swear I'll never forgive you."

Instead of answering, Lane kissed Meg hard. And then she turned and jogged back up the pier. She didn't dare look back in case she lost her nerve. The easiest thing would be to get in the boat with Lois and Meg and head for Boston. But she couldn't do that.

Whatever this thing was that had woken up, she needed to kill it. If she didn't, Lane had no doubt that the sickness would spread across the United States and out into the world. It needed to be stopped now.

❖

Meg sat in the boat and listened to the battle raging out on Commercial. She'd never felt so useless in all her life. She should be out there with Lane, not hiding in a boat.

"You can go if you want. I'll be okay," Lois said.

She couldn't leave her, though. Meg would never forgive herself if something happened to Lois.

"It's okay, honey. Lane will be fine. We'll just wait here for her," Meg said.

Suddenly, there was a loud explosion. Meg looked up to

see the helicopter in a ball of flames, hurtling towards the sea. That couldn't be good. Meg tried not to think about where Lane was and if she'd seen it too.

"Meg, I can hide on the boat. They won't find me. Then you can go and make sure Lane is okay," Lois said again.

Could she, though? Was it totally irresponsible to leave Lois here alone? Probably, but then they weren't exactly in an ideal situation. But Lane was long gone with the magic knife thing, which meant Meg would have to navigate the town alone. It was a risk, and Lane would be furious.

"Okay, get under these life jackets," Meg said. "Don't poke your head out for anyone, and if you see zombies coming up the pier, untie the boat. You're better drifting on the ocean than staying here."

Lois nodded and disappeared behind a wall of bright yellow plastic. Meg picked up the gun Wendy had thoughtfully left lying on the pier and checked the clip. Four rounds left. She hoped that would be enough to get her to Winthrop Street.

CHAPTER EIGHTEEN

Lane stopped once to look behind her. The military was back, and this time there were more of them. A lot more of them. The town looked like something out of an action movie.

Zombies were being mown down, blown up, and torn apart all over the place. The problem was, most of them were getting back up. "You have to hit them in the head," Lane whispered to herself. She wanted to go over and tell them so, but she knew she'd end up getting shot or run over herself.

The best thing for everyone would be if she managed to get to Winthrop Street and rebury the treasure. If that didn't stop the rampage, it would surely bring Sigmarsson back, and then she would try to kill him.

As though thinking about him summoned him, he was suddenly in the middle of the street. Lane winced as he shot blue flames out of his mouth and sent a tank flipping over and over up the road like a toy. This was what she was up against. It didn't look good for her.

Lane hurried on up the road. She made sure to keep looking back in case Sigmarsson saw her and decided to come after her. He must know she was still about. And that she had the power to hurt him. Or rather, the knife did.

"Lane."

Lane stopped. It sounded like Meg calling her name. But that was impossible. Meg was back at the boat with Lois.

"Lane!"

Lane turned and there she was. Lane was equal parts furious and relieved.

"What are you doing here?" Lane asked.

"What do you think? I've come to help you," Meg said.

"Why?"

"Like you said, I'm the other hero in this movie. I can't very well hide out in a boat, can I?"

Lane laughed. "You might die."

Meg shrugged. "It's fifty-fifty."

Behind them, another explosion. Lane spun round in time to see Sigmarsson wrestling with something his own size. Behind them, a truck was in flames.

For a second, she thought the thing Sigmarsson was wrestling with was some kind of military weapon, but it couldn't be that. Then she realized…

"Meg, is that a *second* chief zombie?"

"Yeah, I think so. Wait, is it Wendy?" Meg asked.

Lane squinted and tried to focus. Between the smoke billowing from the wrecked truck and the lousy light, it was hard to make out just who Sigmarsson was fighting with.

Then Lane saw it. Or, rather, saw her. It was Wendy. Somehow she'd come back and, in true Wendy style, not just as a run-of-the-mill zombie, but as a zombie to match the size and power of Ivar Sigmarsson.

Lane clutched the strap of the bag she was carrying. Did this have something to do with the treasure inside? Once you had ownership of it, you found it impossible to let it go?

She thought it might. You didn't have to look far to see examples throughout history, in every place on earth, of the lengths people would go to possess *things*. People were slaughtered by the thousands, rainforests decimated, rivers poisoned.

Lane wondered—if it came to it, would she be able to give the treasure up? Or would some human instinct prevent her from doing it? The knife held a lot of power, and the treasure would make her rich in her own right.

Meg squeezed her arm. "Lane, are you all right?"

Lane nodded. "Yeah, it's Wendy."

Because Wendy'd only been dead a short time, she wasn't as decomposed as Sigmarsson. But she was ravaged. Lane guessed from the pasting she'd gotten on the pier. She was still too far away to see properly but could make out that much of Wendy's throat was missing. It turned her stomach.

"We'd better get out of here before they see us," Meg said.

Lane nodded. "Yes, we should."

❖

Meg led the way down Bradford. They'd had to cut up here because of World War III down on Commercial between Wendy, Sigmarsson, and the US military.

It was strangely quiet. The sky was growing darker again—not that there was much difference between day and night right now.

The wind was picking up, and Meg was cold. She pulled her jacket tight around herself.

"Cold?" Lane asked from behind her.

Meg glanced back and smiled. "A little. Also tired. It's been a long couple days."

"It has," was all Lane said.

They were here. Meg turned right at Winthrop Street.

The house hadn't been touched since the treasure was dug up. A bulldozer sat idle on a patch of bare earth and rubble, a deep trench in front of it.

The house was framed but nothing else had been done. It must be costing the owner a fortune in delays. Or maybe not any more. Maybe the owner had gone the way of most of the residents in Provincetown.

Meg thought about all the people who lived and worked in town. How many were still alive? How many were walking around enduring a fate worse than death?

"Meg, is this it? Are we here?" Lane asked quietly.

"Yeah. We're here."

"And that hole in the ground?"

"I'm pretty sure that's where they dug up the Viking treasure," Meg said. She'd been down to the site like everyone else to look, on the day it happened.

"This is it then. I'd better hurry," Lane said in an understated way that made Meg laugh.

"I guess we'd better."

They climbed down into the ditch together. Lane took the bag off her shoulders.

"Should I just tip it out?" Lane asked.

"As opposed to what?"

"I don't know, place it gently in the dirt."

"Why does it matter?" Meg asked.

"I suppose it doesn't," Lane said.

All the same she knelt in the dirt and carefully emptied the bag out. "It's lovely," she said.

Meg agreed. The jewellery was delicate. The light was bad, but even so, Meg could see how beautiful some of the pieces were.

"It's such a shame to just bury it in the dirt," Meg said.

With the money from this stuff, she could buy a couple

bars—or not work at all. She could spend the rest of her days in luxury.

But that would mean risking the lives of everyone on the Cape and probably in the world.

Ivar Sigmarsson had to be stopped. There was nothing to say he would rest when he got back his treasure. Which was why Lane had the knife.

"You still have the knife, right?" Meg asked Lane, suddenly panicked.

"Don't worry, I have it here." Lane lifted her shirt and Meg saw the handle of the knife sticking up from her waistband.

"Okay, good. Now what?" Meg asked.

"I suppose we wait."

"For him to come back?"

"Yes. We should be prepared for Wendy to come with him," Lane said.

"I don't doubt she will. This treasure was her obsession in life, and I don't imagine much has changed now that she's—" Meg abruptly stopped speaking.

"Quick, out of the ditch," Lane said and they scrambled out.

In the distance, Meg could hear something coming.

❖

Lane heard the low sound of moaning. It wasn't one or two moans, but it sounded like hundreds. She crouched behind the bulldozer with Meg and waited. Against her side the knife felt warm.

"It's pulsing," she whispered to Meg. "It knows they're coming."

"Good. Then it's ready. Are we?" Meg asked.

"Yes. I'm ready. Meg?"

"Yes?"

"I love you," Lane said. It felt good. She didn't think it would ever get old, telling Meg she loved her.

"I love you too," Meg replied.

Lane whipped her head around. Meg just told her she loved her. Did she mean it in the way Lane did, or was it more something she was saying because there was a good possibility they were both about to die? Was it more of an end-of-the-world type *I love you*?

Whatever it was, it felt good. And now was really not the time to be thinking about it because Sigmarsson was here with an entourage of about fifty zombies.

"Fuck," was all Lane said.

She guessed this was it. All her life had been spent pleasing herself. No responsibility and no consequences. How different her life had turned out to be. If this was how it was going to end, she was glad it would end with her finally doing something that counted. And even if she was to die, she would die trying her best to make sure Meg survived.

Lane took a deep breath, turned and kissed Meg on the cheek, then stood up. She walked out from behind the bulldozer with the langseax held tightly in her hand. It burned. And so did her left arse cheek, which was great. It had probably cramped up while she'd been crouched behind the construction equipment. Just what she needed.

"Erm, hey, you," Lane said.

Sigmarsson's gaze was fixed on the trench and most likely the treasure lying in it. At the sound of Lane's voice he turned, and his milky dead eyes locked onto hers.

"Arn," he said. Or at least that's what it sounded like. Lane remembered her hallucination back on Commercial Street when she'd first picked up the knife.

"My name is Lane," she said. "We've given you back your treasure, and now we want you to…I don't know, be at peace?" She hadn't really rehearsed what she'd say to him. "Basically, we want you to get back in your grave. Please."

Sigmarsson laughed. Lane felt stupid. This wasn't how things went in the movies. Everyone knew exactly what to say and didn't sound at all ridiculous.

"Die," was all Sigmarsson said.

He lifted his arms, and his horde began to move towards Lane. She lifted the knife, and the horde shrank back.

Lane took a step forward, and the horde shuffled back. Several bumped into each other, fell over, or bit out at each other. They were confused, afraid.

Suddenly, Sigmarsson opened his mouth and let out a screech. Wisps of blue smoke started to swirl around him becoming denser and getting faster until he sucked it all in, and then fired it back out at Lane in a long stream of blue fire.

Out of instinct, Lane dived left but quickly realized she wasn't fully out of the way. She wielded the knife like a bat and swung.

The blue fire hit the knife, and the force of it sent shock waves up her arm. Shit, that hurt. Lane landed painfully on her side but didn't take her eyes off the blue fire which seemed to fragment and then separate, turning back into wisps of harmless smoke again.

But before she could get back up, Sigmarsson was upon her. He grabbed her by her shirt and lifted her up. This close, she could smell the rotten, fetid stench coming off him. He shouldn't smell like this, she thought. He was just dust and bones by now.

Lane kicked out her legs and managed to catch Ivar hard in what was left of his stomach. He didn't flinch. He started to open his mouth again, and Lane knew this was it, curtains, if she didn't do something.

"Hey, asshole."

Meg.

Sigmarsson turned his head. Lane looked past his shoulder to where Meg stood, waving her arms.

"Meg, no," Lane shouted.

Meg ignored her. "Come on, over here."

Lane raised her arm and tightened her grip on the knife.

"That's right, come and get me," Meg shouted again.

As Lane brought the knife down, Sigmarsson turned his head back around to face her.

He let go of her shirt and, with one huge hand, reached out and grabbed the wrist of the hand that held the knife. He squeezed, and Lane felt something snap.

The pain was unbearable. She cried out, and white spots danced in front of her eyes.

She dropped the knife.

The world receded.

She was going to die.

Her arse cheek still burned. And then she remembered.

With her good hand, Lane reached into her back pocket. It was there, the card. She pulled it out.

It was on fire.

Going purely on instinct and with no real idea why, Lane held the tarot card out—the one which depicted her as a warrior—and then slammed it into Sigmarsson's forehead.

He screeched and dropped her.

Lane hit the ground hard. Pain flared in her hip, but she did her best to ignore it as she rolled away and got onto her feet.

The knife had landed several feet away from her. Sigmarsson was still screeching and clutching his forehead.

But just as Lane went to grab the knife, she was shoved to the ground. Hard.

She looked up, and standing over her was Wendy—or a version of Wendy, at least. Wendy stood about seven feet tall, like Sigmarsson.

For a moment, Wendy stared at her, and Lane was certain she was going to kill her. Then she seemed to change her mind.

Wendy turned and faced Sigmarsson. She opened her mouth and fired a bolt of blue straight at him.

Lane scrambled for the knife.

She reached it at the same time as Meg.

"Well, this was unexpected," Lane said to her.

Meg grinned. "To say the least. Come on, let's get out of the way of these two."

They dived for cover back behind the bulldozer.

Over by the trench, Wendy looked to be getting the better of Sigmarsson. The card Lane had hit him with had left a deep scorch mark on his leathery head, and Wendy's blue bolt another across his chest.

Sigmarsson screeched again, and his horde of zombies surged forward, biting and tearing at Wendy.

"How did she come back like him and not like them?" Meg whispered beside Lane.

"I don't know. I suppose she's the same as him. So desperate for that treasure. She'll do anything to get it."

"I guess. How's your wrist?" Meg asked.

"It's okay. I mean, it's very broken, but it's okay."

The truth was it was agony. It throbbed and made Lane feel sick, but she was still alive, so she couldn't complain too much.

Over by the trench, Sigmarsson lunged at Wendy. Together with his horde, he took her to the ground. She screeched. The horde fell upon her, ripping and tearing.

This is it, thought Lane. *My one chance. My only chance.*

Sigmarsson tore Wendy's head from her shoulders, and then he held it aloft. He gathered a huge bolt of blue fire, and Wendy's head was consumed.

Her body lay still.

She was finally truly dead.

Lane took a deep breath, gathered her courage, and charged out from behind the bulldozer.

Sigmarsson turned just as she dived at him.

For a second, Lane thought she might not make it.

He tried to twist around, but it was too late.

Lane buried the knife between his shoulders.

Sigmarsson screeched, but this time it was full of pain and fury. Lane twisted the knife and pulled it out. She stabbed him again.

He swatted her off like a fly, and she fell backwards. Stunned, she couldn't move. And then he was upon her.

Lane angled the knife so the blade was away from her. As he bore down, Lane thrust up.

The knife sank deep into the place where his heart would have been were he a living man.

Lane squeezed her eyes shut and waited. He let out one final screech that deafened her and sent pain through her ears and straight into her brain.

And then he was still.

Lane rolled away from him and did her best to stand. Somewhere behind her, Meg screamed.

❖

Meg always thought the phrase *frozen with fear* was a stupid one. How could anybody be frozen with fear?

When she saw Lane lying on the ground and Sigmarsson bearing down on her, she finally understood. Her feet were rooted to the spot, and her mind was emptied of all thought except *Please don't die, please don't die.*

When Sigmarsson screeched, and she saw Lane roll away from him, she was dizzy with relief—and there was another phrase she'd never understood until this moment.

But as quickly as relief replaced fear, fear found its way back to her almost immediately.

She'd all but forgotten about the zombie horde waiting patiently near their master. And now that he was dead, they began to move.

At first, it was just one or two. They looked like they were dancing some crazy kind of jig. Their feet shuffled, and they held their arms down at their sides like they were in *Riverdance.* Then the first one's head exploded. Like, literally burst open.

As though the others had seen it and thought, *Yeah, that looks like a cool idea*, they started to dance too, and then their heads started to explode. Meg couldn't help it. She screamed.

"Meg, Meg, are you okay?"

Meg hadn't noticed Lane had come to stand beside her, she'd been so horribly fixated on the exploding zombies.

"Yeah, sorry I screamed. Are you seeing this?" Meg asked.

"Yeah, and I have to say, I'm sort of relieved. I didn't fancy fighting them off with just one good arm," Lane replied.

"But why are they doing it?" Meg couldn't take her eyes off them. "And why are you calm about it?"

"I believe the word is *numb*. I feel numb. Except my wrist, which is killing me. The exploding zombie heads? They don't surprise me. Sigmarsson was the one creating them and keeping them together. I guess without him, they can't survive either."

Meg watched as another head exploded. Bodies littered the ground where they fell. It was awful. Once, these had been people. Her neighbours. Meg hadn't exactly been close to anyone in Provincetown, but she'd known a lot of them and now they were dead—or dying. She guessed it was better this way than living some in-between life as a zombie.

"Meg?"

Meg felt Lane's hand on her shoulder. "I know. We should get back to Lois and make sure she's okay."

"Come on. There's nothing we can do for them."

Meg nodded. Lane was right. But all the same, it seemed so sad and almost wrong to just leave them here like this. She guessed the military would come along and pick them up, probably incinerate them. You couldn't exactly bury zombies.

"Meg?" Lane said again.

"Okay, I'm coming."

Back on Commercial Street, the place was deserted. There were signs the military had been here—burned out trucks and even a tank. Otherwise, the place was dead.

Meg guessed that made sense when most of the inhabitants of the town were dead.

She realized she hadn't given Lane a hug or a kiss or thanked her for saving her life back there.

"Lane, thank you." Meg stopped in the street and turned. "I know thank you is inadequate for what you did but—"

Lane silenced her with a kiss.

"Meg, we both did it. You drew him away from me when he would have killed me. We did it together."

Meg guessed that was true. That, at least, felt good. They'd stopped the zombie horde from spreading.

"It just seems so strange, though, all the zombies just dying. Even if he made them and could control them, *they* bit people—people I knew—and turned them into zombies," Meg said.

"Meg, it's over." Lane pulled Meg into her arms and held her tight. "It's over."

Meg leaned into Lane and closed her eyes. She really wanted that to be true.

"Let's go and get Lois," Lane said.

Meg nodded and they started walking again.

On the pier, Meg was relieved to see no fresh blood.

"Lois?" she called when they reached the boat, which was still tied to the dock. "Lois, you can come out now. It's over."

The yellow life jackets rippled and then fell away as Lois got up. "Swear? They're all gone?" the little girl asked.

Meg held out her arms. "I swear."

Lois leaped off the boat with a shout. "Lane did it! Lane killed the zombies."

Lane laughed and ruffled Lois's hair as Lois threw herself into Meg's arms. "I didn't do it alone. Meg helped a bit."

Meg looked at Lane over Lois's head. "A bit?"

Lane made a pinching sign with two fingers on her good hand. "A smidgen."

"Oh, really? Sigmarsson was about to kick your ass until I helped you a *bit*," Meg said and laughed.

Lane pretended to look affronted, and Lois giggled. "That's not true at all. I definitely had him on the ropes. Don't listen to her, Lois."

Meg rolled her eyes. "Whatever, Lane. Come on, let's get out of here. I think if we walk up Bradford, we might run into the military at some point."

Meg held out her hands and Lane and Lois took one each. They walked back down the pier hand in hand.

❖

Outer Cape Echo
5 minutes ago

It's zombies. Get off the Cape while you can.

523 Likes   *3 Comments*

Will Roach: Is this some kind of joke?

Gemma Ward: They must have been hacked.

Mike Radford: I don't think so. I've just come back from the grocery store and seen it with my own eyes. You should all get out now while you can.

Lane was exhausted and her wrist was killing her. Not to mention her hip and just about every other bone and muscle in her body. But she hadn't felt this good in years.

After spending most of her life feeling like she was good for pretty much nothing, Lane had proven she was good for something—taking care of her friends. She had courage, and she'd been willing to lay down her life for Meg and Lois and even Wendy before she'd betrayed them—well, she'd been betraying them from the beginning. So maybe not Wendy.

Things were going to change. Whether Meg wanted her or not, Lane was not the same person she had been before she came to Provincetown, and she was going to set about making big changes as soon as they got out of here.

Of course, her family's money was nice, but she didn't need it, had never really needed it. Her family wouldn't be able to hang the trust fund over her head any more. If they didn't like her choices, they could cut her off. It didn't matter any more.

"So, how do you feel about running a bar?"

Meg's question pulled Lane from her thoughts, and at first she didn't really register what she was asking. "A bar? What?"

Meg laughed. "How do you feel about running a bar? With me."

"With you?"

"Damn, Lane, did one of those zombies break your head as well as your wrist? I'm asking if you want to be with me—I'm asking if you'll take me back." Meg laughed again but Lane could see she was nervous.

This whole zombie apocalypse must have changed Meg too because the old Meg would never have made herself so vulnerable.

Lane stopped in the street and pretended to think about it. "Well, I mean, it's a lot of work, this bar business. What's the pay like?"

Meg looked confused for a moment and then grinned. "Not great but there are bonuses." She winked.

"Bonuses? Really? And what about annual leave?"

"Oh, there's tons of vacation—I mean, let's be honest, being with me is a vacation all in itself," Meg said.

"Then how could I refuse?" Lane replied. "Meg, I came halfway across the world for you. I love you."

Meg stepped forward and kissed Lane lightly on the mouth. "And I'm so glad you did. I love you too."

"Gross," Lois piped up.

Lane and Meg laughed. "Watch it, or we'll make you work in the cellar dragging beer barrels," Lane said.

"Will I stay with you, then?" Lois asked.

"I don't know, sweetheart." Lane crouched down and pulled Lois into a hug. "Your aunt might want you to be with her. Either way, we'll see you all the time."

Suddenly, the sound of a revving engine broke the silence.

"What the hell is that?" Meg asked.

"I don't know." Lane lifted Lois into her arms, and they ducked into the mouth of an alley.

The sound of the engine grew louder. In the distance, they could see a multicoloured monstrosity of a car hurtling towards them.

"It's just Dolores," Lois said.

Lane quickly dashed into the road and waved her arms in the hope Dolores might see them and slow down.

The car swerved to the kerb and braked sharply. The passenger window rolled down with a squeak.

"Boyd, isn't it?" came the familiar voice from within.

Lane bent down by the window. "It is. I've got Meg Daltry and Lois with me."

"Huh. I wouldn't have pegged you to be one of the ones who made it," Dolores said.

"Thanks a lot," Lane said.

"I was up in Wellfleet visiting my sister. The army had this whole place sealed off. I only just got back in."

"They just let you back in?" Lane asked. That didn't sound right.

"Didn't have much choice. Got their hands full up and down the Cape," Dolores said.

Just then, a handful of jets passed overhead. Lane watched them go.

"What's going on, Dolores?" Lane asked, afraid of the answer.

"Whatever happened here in Provincetown, it got out. It

was all over the Cape. People going zombie everywhere you looked. Then the damnedest thing happened."

"You're saying there are more zombies?" Meg had come over and was clutching Lois's hand tightly.

"Were. *Were* more zombies. I was coming back here for my guns and supplies. Thought to head inland. Then those bastards just lay down and died. Right there on the ground. Never seen anything like it in my whole life." Dolores went silent for a moment, as if remembering. Then she shook herself, and it was as if she was seeing them and the state they were in for the first time. "You want a ride? Might be better than walking. You all look terrible," Dolores said.

Lane couldn't quite believe it. If not for them and the langseax, those zombies—the ones who got out—could be rampaging across North America right now. She felt relief. Huge relief. They'd done the right thing.

"You want a ride or not? I got to get out of here," Dolores said.

"Yes, we want a ride," Meg said and opened the rear door. She helped Lois inside. "Come on, Lane. We've got a bar to buy."

Lane climbed in the car. Whatever else happened, they had each other. And the knife. And Lois. Most important of all she had Meg, and together they were going to be okay. Whatever came next, Lane wasn't letting Meg go a second time.

Dolores shifted the car into gear and gunned the engine. "Buckle up, kids," she said. "I don't drive below forty, and I'm hoping to use a couple of those dead zombies as speed bumps on my way through."

Lane put her seat belt on.

Whatever happened next, she'd face it with Meg at her

side, and there was no one in the world she'd rather have there. Meg was the other hero, after all.

Lane reached back with her good hand, and Meg took it. "I love you," Lane said.

Meg squeezed Lane's hand. "And I love you. Dolores, get us the fuck out of here."

About the Author

Eden Darry is freshly minted resident of Kent, having previously been a lifelong Londoner. She lives with her partner and no pets (yet) and has two novels published with Bold Strokes Books—*The House* and *Vanished*.

Books Available From Bold Strokes Books

Best Practice by Carsen Taite. When attorney Grace Maldonado agrees to mentor her best friend's little sister, she's prepared to confront Perry's rebellious nature, but she isn't prepared to fall in love. Legal Affairs: one law firm, three best friends, three chances to fall in love. (978-1-63555-361-1)

Home by Kris Bryant. Natalie and Sarah discover that anything is possible when love takes the long way home. (978-1-63555-853-1)

Keeper by Sydney Quinne. With a new charge under her reluctant wing—feisty, highly intelligent math wizard Isabelle Templeton—Keeper Andy Bouchard has to prevent a murder or die trying. (978-1-63555-852-4)

One More Chance by Ali Vali. Harry Bastantes planned a future with Desi Thompson until the day Desi disappeared without a word, only to walk back into her life sixteen years later. (978-1-63555-536-3)

Renegade's War by Gun Brooke. Freedom fighter Aurelia DeCallum regrets saving the woman called Blue. She fears it will jeopardize her mission, and secretly, Blue might end up breaking Aurelia's heart. (978-1-63555-484-7)

The Other Women by Erin Zak. What happens in Vegas should stay in Vegas, but what do you do when the love you find in Vegas changes your life forever? (978-1-63555-741-1)

The Sea Within by Missouri Vaun. Time is running out for Dr. Elle Graham to convince Captain Jackson Drake that the only thing that can save future Earth resides in the past, and rescue her broken heart in the process. (978-1-63555-568-4)

To Sleep With Reindeer Justine Saracen. In Norway under Nazi occupation, Maarit, an Indigenous woman, and Kirsten, a Norwegian resister, join forces to stop the development of an atomic weapon. (978-1-63555-735-0)

Twice Shy by Aurora Rey. Having an ex with benefits isn't all it's cracked up to be. Will Amanda Russo learn that lesson in time to take a chance on love with Quinn Sullivan? (978-1-63555-737-4)

Z-Town by Eden Darry. Forced to work together to stay alive, Meg and Lane must find the centuries-old treasure before the zombies find them first. (978-1-63555-743-5)

Bet Against Me by Fiona Riley. In the high-stakes luxury real estate market, everything has a price, and as rival Realtors Trina Lee and Kendall Yates find out, that means their hearts and souls, too. (978-1-63555-729-9)

Broken Reign by Sam Ledel. Together on an epic journey in search of a mysterious cure, a princess and a village outcast must overcome life-threatening challenges and their own prejudice if they want to survive. (978-1-63555-739-8)

Just One Taste by CJ Birch. For Lauren, it only took one taste to start trusting in love again. (978-1-63555-772-5)

Lady of Stone by Barbara Ann Wright. Sparks fly as a magical emergency forces a noble embarrassed by her ability to submit to a low-born teacher who resents everything about her. (978-1-63555-607-0)

Last Resort by Angie Williams. Katie and Rhys are about to find out what happens when you meet the girl of your dreams but you aren't looking for a happily ever after. (978-1-63555-774-9)

Longing for You by Jenny Frame. When Debrek housekeeper Katie Brekman is attacked amid a burgeoning vampire-witch war, Alexis Villiers must go against everything her clan believes in to save her. (978-1-63555-658-2)

Money Creek by Anne Laughlin. Clare Lehane is a troubled lawyer from Chicago who tries to make her way in a rural town full of secrets and deceptions. (978-1-63555-795-4)

Passion's Sweet Surrender by Ronica Black. Cam and Blake are unable to deny their passion for each other, but surrendering to love is a whole different matter. (978-1-63555-703-9)

The Holiday Detour by Jane Kolven. It will take everything going wrong to make Dana and Charlie see how right they are for each other. (978-1-63555-720-6)

CPSIA information can be obtained
at www.ICGtesting.com
Printed in the USA
LVHW041011110621
689906LV00004B/246

9 781635 557435